Happy Reading!

IN OVER HER HEAD

TERRI OSBURN

Terri
xoxo

Macie Rae
PUBLISHING

OTHER BOOKS BY TERRI OSBURN

Anchor Island Series

Meant To Be

Up To The Challenge

Home To Stay

More To Give

In Over Her Head

Christmas On Anchor Island*

*coming Oct 2021

Ardent Springs Series

His First And Last

Our Now And Forever

My One And Only

Her Hopes And Dreams

The Last In Love

Shooting Stars Series

Rising Star

Falling Star

Wishing On A Star

Among The Stars

Stand-Alones
Ask Me To Stay
Wrecked
Awakening Anna

WHEN SHE'D DREAMED OF HER FIRST RESTAURANT, Lauren Riley had imagined a dining room filled with delicious scents that would make diners' mouths water. She had not pictured an empty space that reeked of paint fumes. And yet, here she was.

"Is the lighthouse really short and fat like that?" Lauren asked the artist, who was dabbing in a small shrub in front of the post office. This was giving her childhood flashbacks to when she'd watched Bob Ross whip up a gorgeous fall landscape with a few flicks of his wrist.

They'd been too poor to afford cable so PBS had been the go-to channel for PG entertainment.

The painting project had been going for a week, which made Mia Stamatis the only person Lauren had spent any real time with since arriving on Anchor Island. She seemed kind, was definitely talented, and most importantly, was not annoying. Lauren didn't do chitchat, nor was she interested in gossip. Mia had offered neither.

Stepping back, she surveyed her work. "Do you think it's *too* fat?"

Lauren leaned against the doorframe where she stood between the kitchen and dining room. "Hell if I know. I haven't seen it."

Green eyes cut Lauren's way. "You haven't seen the lighthouse yet?"

"I've only been on the island for two weeks," she defended.

She'd come to Anchor Island to be head chef at Pilar's—previously known as the Marina restaurant— and overseeing the renovation took top priority. The sooner they opened the doors, the sooner she could get back to cooking, and in Lauren's mind that could not happen soon enough.

The owner of the place, Will Navarro, had specific ideas that didn't necessarily gel with Lauren's. Will was all about celebrating the island. Lauren preferred to celebrate her food. She'd reminded herself more than once that Will was the one footing the bill, and if she wanted a giant mural of her precious island, then she should have one. In the end, patrons would be too busy admiring their plates to notice the wall, but Lauren had kept that fact to herself.

"Have you taken any time to sightsee?" Mia asked.

The thought hadn't even occurred to her. "I'm not on vacation. I'm here to work."

"That means you're also here to live. Don't you want to know more about your new home?"

Home. Not a word Lauren knew much about. During her childhood, she, Mom, and her younger brother Knox had fled or been evicted from more places than she could count. Since Lauren had struck out on her own at nineteen, she'd lived in apartments, townhouses, and two weeks ago had moved into what some might deem a charming island cottage.

These had all been places to store her stuff. None of them she'd ever considered a home. The island cottage was also the first time she had a place all to herself, and only because it was a perk of the job.

"I'll get around eventually."

Lauren had already discovered the important locations. The small grocer who carried more fresh food than she'd expected. The Hava Java coffee shop where she got her morning fix. And the gym, where she worked out at least an hour a day six days a week.

Kitchen work took stamina and focus, both of which required keeping her mind and body in tip-top shape. Lucky for her, the restaurant owners also owned the fitness center and had thrown in a complementary membership as part of her benefits package.

Mia dropped her paint brush into a plastic cup of water and reached for a towel to wipe her hands. "If you want a tour guide, I'd be happy to show you around. The island is small but there's still plenty to see."

"I doubt I'll have time before we get this place opened."

"That's fair," Mia said, "but the offer stands whenever you're ready." She took two steps back from the wall and once again assessed her work. "I think this puppy might be done."

"Might be?" Lauren asked. Shouldn't she know one way or the other?

Head tilted, Mia shrugged. "I could tweak it forever and never consider it finished, but in this case, Will is the one who gets to decide." Turning to face Lauren, she said, "Do you know what time it is?"

Lauren checked her watch. "Two fifty-five."

"Perfect. Nick should be here any minute."

"I'm already here," boomed a voice from the entrance. Lauren spun to find an elderly woman shuffle in with the help of a bright-blue cane and followed by the cook from Dempsey's.

Lauren met Nick Stamatis the day after arriving on the island and hadn't given him much thought since. He had an attitude, but nothing she wasn't used to. As a woman in a male-dominated field, Lauren had dealt with her share of bullies, blowhards, and flat-out bastards. Nick hadn't qualified in any of those categories, at least not during their brief encounter, but he *had* shown a not-so-subtle aversion to a new chef entering his territory.

"Grandma, come and tell me what you think," Mia called out to the new arrivals. She crossed the room and slipped a hand beneath the older woman's arm to help her along. "I just finished."

"Let me make sure you didn't miss anything," the woman said, leaning heavily on the cane as they crossed the room.

While the grandmother perused the artwork, her escort cut a glance Lauren's way. She lifted a brow in greeting. Not until several days into the mural work did Lauren learn that the cook was Mia's older brother. She'd mentioned earlier that they were celebrating Nick's birthday later in the day. Though he didn't look like a man about to celebrate anything.

With dark brows locked over whiskey-brown eyes, he ran a hand through his black hair and scowled as his gaze returned to his family members. With nothing else to do, Lauren observed Nick unnoticed. Any woman with a pulse would say he was attractive, but something else about him caught her attention.

Nick Stamatis possessed every inch he occupied. And he occupied a lot. The faded jeans did wonders for his ass, or maybe the other way around, and the well-worn jacket hung off wide shoulders. She imagined he commanded respect in the kitchen and wondered not for the first time if that was a skill one could learn or if they had to be born with it.

She yearned for that kind of power. The kind that no one could question.

Her assessment was cut short when Nick walked her way.

"I hear you're revamping this place."

"I am," she replied as he drew closer.

His hands slid into the pockets of his jacket as his eyes cut to the brightly lit space behind her. "That kitchen was pretty old. Is Will giving you a new one?"

"The renovation includes the kitchen, yeah. Most of the new equipment is in place, but the sixty-inch range is on back order so that's holding things up." If the range had been on time, they might have been able to open earlier than planned. Now they'd be lucky to make the month-end relaunch date.

"Then you aren't reopening May first?"

A detail of their plan she hadn't thought was out yet in case a delay was needed. That was one of the cons about moving to such a small community—everyone knew everyone else's business whether you wanted them to or not.

"That's still more than three weeks away so we shouldn't have any problem hitting the date," she lied.

There were several items that had yet to arrive. Anchor Island wasn't just a small community. It was a barrier island only accessible via ferry, and that apparently slowed down deliveries. Lauren had never been a patient person so this entire process felt like a test.

"Grandma, this is the friend I was telling you about." Mia smiled as Lauren looked her way. She wouldn't say they were friends, but correcting the statement seemed rude. "Lauren Riley, this is Nota Stamatis, our grandmother."

"Nice to meet you, Mrs. Stamatis."

The older woman leaned both hands on the top of her cane. "Likewise, my dear, but Mrs. Stamatis was my mother-in-law. Dreadful woman. Call me Nota." Tapping Mia with her elbow, she added, "You said she was pretty, and you were right."

"When did I say that?" Mia asked, her cheeks turning pink.

"You were on the phone with someone. I overheard."

"That's called eavesdropping," Nick scolded.

Dark eyes that appeared to run in the family sparkled with mischief. "I was in the next room. What was I supposed to do? Not listen?"

"Yes," the siblings said in unison.

The Stamatis matriarch looked unaffected. "Nick is a cook, too," she said to Lauren. "And single."

The man in question rolled his eyes as his sister said, "We should go."

"He isn't just any cook," Nota continued. "He's won Best of the Fest two years in a row."

Now they had her attention.

"Best of the Fest?" Lauren repeated. "What is that?"

"Anchor Island has an annual food festival in May," Mia explained. "Several prizes are awarded, including the food voted Best of the Fest from all participating restaurants."

Why hadn't Will mentioned this? "Is that limited to island eateries?"

"Restaurants up and down the coast participate," Nick answered. "From Corolla on down. The winner gets a feature in *Food & Fare* magazine."

This would be the perfect way to introduce herself as one of the best chefs in the area, and to bring attention to the restaurant. Winning recipes started racing through her mind. "Then Pilar's will participate as well."

"Not an option," Nick said.

The hell it wasn't. "Why not?"

"Because Will is on the festival committee," Mia explained. "It's considered a conflict of interest."

That was easily fixed. "Then she'll get off the committee."

Three sets of eyes blinked as if Lauren had suggested her boss be killed.

"Will created the festival," Nota said. "She would never step away. This event is her baby."

No way in hell would Lauren sit on the sidelines while every restaurant on the coast competed for best food. Yes, her menu alone would bring in customers—eventually. Winning this prize and getting national coverage would bring them now. She needed this in order to prove that she belonged in the kitchen, contrary to what some in her past would say.

"We'll see about that," Lauren said.

An awkward silence fell over the foursome until Mia

said, "Well, we have a birthday to celebrate. Grandma, give me two minutes to clean up and I'll be ready to go."

"Take your time, dear."

"Happy birthday," Lauren said to Nick. She'd spent her last four birthdays alone. It must have been nice to have even this small family unit with whom to celebrate.

"Thanks." Changing the subject, he said, "When are you bringing the staff back?"

Lauren had yet to pick her team. "We'll be holding interviews next week."

His weight shifted as he rose to his full height and faced her head-on. Lauren was five ten, but Nick had her by at least four inches, and his shoulders suddenly blocked the entire entrance.

"What's wrong with the staff you have?"

"I just told you I don't have a staff." If he thought a challenging stance would intimidate her, he was mistaken. "Once I conduct interviews, I'll build a competent crew. I need people who know their way around a kitchen. Not a fry cook and a grill runner."

"The Marina staff know more about this kitchen and this island than you do," he informed her. "Letting them go would be a mistake."

"They don't know *my* kitchen."

"They can learn."

"I'll find that out in the interviews then, won't I?"

With furrowed brows, he stared her down for several seconds. "This is a tight-knit community," he finally said. "We take care of our own, and that means we hire our own. Don't make assumptions about us, and if you want this place to succeed, don't make enemies before you open the doors."

Undaunted, Lauren raised a brow. "I didn't say I wouldn't hire locals, and I also didn't ask for your advice."

To her surprise, Nota laughed. "You two would make an excellent match. You're exactly alike."

Lauren doubted either statement was true. "I have more calls to make," she said, nodding toward the older woman. "I hope to see you again once we're open. I have a lamb chop recipe I think you'd enjoy."

Long before culinary school, Lauren had possessed a talent for knowing the food a person would like just from meeting them. Her assumptions were rarely wrong.

"I'm looking forward to it, my dear."

"All done," Mia said, rejoining them. "Lauren, I left my supplies in the storage room like before in case Will wants any changes. Once she gives her final approval, I'll take it all home."

"Not a problem."

Nick escorted Nota to the door while Mia lingered behind. "I want to apologize for my grandmother. She's determined to see Nick and I married off, and unfortunately, that puts her in constant mate-recruitment mode. You know how grandmothers are."

Lauren never met either of her grandmothers, so no, she didn't know.

"She seems nice." A glance toward the door revealed how tightly Nota clung to her grandson's arm, and how carefully he ushered her along, as if she might break at the slightest misstep. "You're lucky to have her."

"We are," Mia agreed. "Thanks for being so nice this week. That tour guide offer still stands. Maybe a little sightseeing will inspire items for your menu."

Keeping her response noncommittal, she said, "Maybe. Have a nice evening."

"You, too."

Mia caught up with her family at the door and they disappeared together into the sunshine. A stab of jealousy sliced through Lauren, but she swept it away with a deep sigh and went back to her office.

———

"I TOLD you we didn't need to do this," Nick said as Mia lowered a birthday cake onto Nota's kitchen table. He made the same claim every year, but this time he meant it. This was the last birthday he felt like celebrating. An apropos thought considering this could also be his *last* birthday ever.

"And we ignored you," Mia replied, "like we always do."

His sister had an annoying habit of ignoring pretty much everything he said. From his birthday to her coming clean with their grandmother.

"Get the candles from the drawer," Nota ordered.

Though his grandmother had claimed she felt fine, her arthritis must have been acting up. She'd plopped into a chair the moment they'd entered the house when normally she'd shoo them out of her kitchen and insist on doing everything herself.

"I don't need candles," Nick said.

"Everyone needs candles," Nota informed him. "When are you going to stop giving us a hard time about your birthday?"

When he stopped having them, Nick thought, but kept the morbid statement to himself.

Mia stuck pink, yellow, blue, and purple candles along the perimeter of the cake and then used a match to light them. "You're going to have another fifty of these things," she said.

He would be lucky to have another four. Nick turned thirty-six this year. His father died at thirty-seven. His grandfather at thirty-nine. His great-grandfather had been killed in World War II at the age of twenty-six, but probably wouldn't have seen forty even if he'd survived. Stamatis men simply did not live to old age. Or middle age, for that matter.

"You two need to face reality," he argued.

His sister blew out the match. "And you need to think positively."

Right. Because that would help him cheat death.

"Start the song, Mia," Nota said, and the pair sang the traditional tune in perfect harmony. When the song ended, they both said, "Make a wish!"

The only thing Nick wished was that the women in his life would stop pretending, but to make them happy, he closed his eyes and did the pretending for them. Seconds later, he opened his eyes and blew out the candles.

Mia passed him the knife and three paper plates. "Do you really like the mural, Grandma?"

Nick had stopped calling Nota grandma years ago, but Mia never lost the habit. He meant no disrespect. She was simply Nota to him. Other than Mia, his paternal grandmother was the most important woman in his life.

His mother had remarried right after Nick graduated high school, and he loved her as any son should, but she'd severed her connection with Dad's side of the family after the second marriage, and then moved to Florida without even discussing the idea with her kids.

"I do," Nota replied. "You brought our beloved island to life on that wall. Everyone is going to love it."

"I hope so."

Once the cake was cut and the pieces distributed, Mia added a scoop of ice cream to each, then they ate in silence until Mia exclaimed, "Your present!" Rising from the table, she rushed off toward the bedrooms down the hall.

"That new chef is beautiful, isn't she?" Nota commented.

She was. She was also a hard-ass with a chip on her

shoulder. Nick knew the type well. A chef with a superiority complex while also being scared shitless. He'd bet his best blades this was her first time running a kitchen. The inexperience was written all over her face. Being able to cook didn't mean a damn thing when it came to managing people. A fact he'd learned long ago.

"Don't get any ideas."

"What?" she mumbled, attempting to look innocent and failing miserably. "I'm just making an observation."

"Like the observation that she and I would make a good match?" Nick had vowed years ago to never date a fellow chef. They were all control freaks with horrible hours, and by nature too damned competitive. He included himself in that summation.

The older woman grinned. "Am I wrong?"

"You are." Other than her profession, Nick knew little about Lauren Riley, but his answer would be the same no matter the woman in question. He never took any relationship beyond casual dating, and what Nota had in mind went well beyond casual.

"Happy birthday," Mia said, returning to the table and setting a photo album down before him.

"What's this?"

She returned to her seat. "Your present."

"Presents are usually wrapped," he pointed out, teasing as he loved to do.

"Consider my drawings wrapping paper," she said before sticking her tongue out at him.

"There are many memories in there," Nota murmured, her eyes focused on the album.

Nick sobered and ran a fingertip over the hand-drawn lettering of their last name. Ironically, a name that literally meant *stop dying*. Tension tightening his chest, he lifted the cover to find the last family picture taken before his father had passed away. A gangly fifteen-year-old Nick stood beside the man who had been everything to him. His hero. His mentor. His biggest fan.

Mia held a similar position beside their mom, lips shut tight to hide the crooked teeth that would land her in braces two years later. He hadn't noticed at the time, but Mom—who was the same age then that Nick was today—looked far older. Her smile looked forced and dark circles lingered beneath her eyes.

Raising two kids while her husband ran the family restaurant had clearly taken a toll.

Behind them loomed the narrow two-story home where Nick had spent every day of his life up to that point. The home he would leave less than a year later as the ill-equipped new man of the family. His gut clenched at the rush of memories. Family-filled holidays. Sunday barbecues. Rare but treasured talks on the squeaky old metal glider on the front porch.

He snapped the cover shut. "I'll look at this later." The two women exchanged a glance but neither pushed. "Thanks for the cake, but I'm going to head out."

Since Mia lived next door, he didn't need to drive

her home. Nick rose from his chair and tucked the album under his arm before walking around to his grandmother and dropping a kiss on her cheek. "Take it easy."

Nota placed a hand along his jawline. "I will." Staring into his eyes, she looked as if she wanted to say something else, but then shook her head and broke the contact. "Don't write that new girl off just yet. I have a good feeling about her."

She had a good feeling about every woman who crossed his path.

Ignoring the statement, he placed a kiss on the top of Mia's head, and then said, "Tell Olaf I said hello."

Olaf Hogenschmidt was a native islander and his grandmother's unofficial male companion for the last year. She doggedly refused to acknowledge anything between them other than friendship, but they behaved more like an old married couple when they didn't think anyone was watching. Nota had never remarried, or even dated as far as Nick knew, after being widowed in her mid-thirties. If Olaf made her happy, then Nick had no problem with the man being in his grandmother's life.

"Who said Olaf is coming over?" Nota asked.

Nick's eyes cut from the cake to his grandmother. "That man can smell cake like a shark senses blood in the water." Snatching his keys from the kitchen counter, he added, "Besides, we both know you invited him."

"I did no such thing," she argued, the claim punctuated by a sudden knock.

Nick crossed the small cottage and opened the front door. "Hey, Olaf. Funny seeing you here."

"I heard there was cake," the older man replied.

Nick stepped back to let him enter. "Yes, there is."

Olaf crossed the threshold, the accompanying scent of pine and varnish revealing he'd come straight from his workshop. With a wave for the ladies at the table, Nick exited the house and closed the door behind him. On the porch, he pulled the album from against his side. The knot in his gut returned, drawing a sigh from deep in his chest.

An important fact had been left out of the conversation inside, as it always was. This wasn't only his birthday. It was his father's as well.

"Happy birthday, Dad." He followed the words with the statement that never left his mind. "I wish you were here."

2

WILL PARSONS WAS HARDER TO PIN DOWN THAN AN octopus in a rainstorm. Lauren had been chasing her around the Destination Anchor office for the last five minutes and was quickly losing patience. The event planning company was another in the Navarro portfolio, and since wedding season was right around the corner, Lauren had been competing for her boss' attention while also spending a significant chunk of her time creating catering menus for events large and small.

"I have to be able to compete," Lauren said for the third time. How was the woman not getting this? "If the festival is as big as I hear, then a win would bring much-needed attention to the restaurant."

The slender woman kept her eyes on the report in her hand. "Roxie, have we confirmed the photographer for the Leland wedding?"

"I sent the email yesterday and if I don't get an answer by tomorrow, I'll give him a call."

Lauren didn't know Will's assistant well, but the younger woman seemed capable. Office attire on Anchor Island leaned much more casual than in Boston, so Roxie's dark jeans and Doc Martens had taken her by surprise. Not many could pull off the punk rock edge and still appear professional, but Roxie Chandler did so with ease.

"Are you listening to me?" Lauren asked, struggling to keep her rising anger in check. "Will, this is important."

Blue eyes finally met hers. "I'm sorry. I'm listening, really I am, but there's nothing I can do. Destination Anchor is a lead sponsor, and I'm the committee chairperson."

"Let someone else be the chairperson this year," Lauren pleaded. "My win could ensure a successful launch for Pilar's."

Will dropped into the chair behind her desk with a heavy sigh. "Lauren, Pilar's will have plenty of publicity regardless of the competition. Four regional publications as well as *Food & Fare* magazine will be covering the event, and I've already lined up interviews with all of them. There'll be three days of activities, during which we'll present dishes ranging from bite-sized hors d'oeuvres to a full main course. We planned the opening for May first precisely to take advantage of the festival. I assure you, the competition is completely unnecessary."

"But I need—"

"You're meeting the Steinmans in ten minutes at the Sunset Harbor Inn," Roxie interrupted, holding out a bright-purple folder. "I've added an updated checklist and a current copy of all costs incurred so far."

"Thanks for the reminder." Will bolted from her chair and snagged a light jacket off the coatrack in the corner. "I'll be back in time to take you to lunch."

"You're meeting Randy at Dempsey's for lunch, remember?"

Hugging the purple folder to her chest, Will glanced toward the ceiling. "What did I ever do without you?"

"You probably missed several meetings," the assistant replied with a smile. "Don't worry about me. Alex is bringing me lunch."

Alex was the straitlaced island doctor whom Lauren had encountered during a previous visit to the Destination Anchor office. She'd never have guessed that Dr. Fielding would be Roxie's type. The two couldn't be more different, at least based on appearances. Lauren's mother had tried the opposites-attract thing with little success, but then her mother had tried every type of guy and they'd all turned out to be losers.

Will set the folder down long enough to pull on the jacket, then grabbed her purse off a different hook and breezed toward the exit. "I'm serious, Lauren. Pilar's will have the best launch possible without you having to worry about that competition."

"But I want to compete," she mumbled as the busy woman left the building.

"She's right," Roxie said. "I get that you're a fighter, but you'll have to sit this one out."

Lauren blinked, curious how a virtual stranger could know such a thing. "Sitting out is not in my vocabulary."

With a chuckle, the assistant tapped the chair in front of her desk before returning to her own. "Sometimes life sucks like that. Have a seat. We need to talk."

Without an excuse to decline, Lauren settled into the chair. "About what?"

Before she could answer, Roxie's cell phone dinged and she checked the screen. A slow smiled curled her lips, but she didn't pause to send a reply. "I'll preface this by saying that I haven't been on the island all that long, but in my short time here, I've learned a thing or two that might help you out."

"I didn't realize I needed help."

"People seldom do." Roxie leaned back in her chair and crossed her arms. "My first suggestion is simple. Relax."

Lauren tensed. "Excuse me?"

"Loosen up. You're on island time now. If you keep giving off that ice queen vibe, you're going to have a hard time fitting in."

Suppressing a growl, Lauren said, "Why would I want to fit in?"

Roxie ignored the open hostility. "Why wouldn't you?"

Because fitting in meant making friends, and Lauren preferred to avoid that activity.

Turning the tables, she said, "*You* don't look like the fit in type."

The woman's smile grew wide. "I know, right? I walked onto this speck of sand with a chip on my shoulder the size of my Camaro." Dark hair swayed as her head tilted to the right. "There's just something about the people here. They don't care who you are or what you've done. If you're here and you pull your weight, then before you know it, you're one of them."

"What if I don't want to be one of them?"

"I'll repeat my question. Why wouldn't you?"

Lauren didn't answer and Roxie took her silence as encouragement.

"There's no reason, right? I mean, you're going to be living here. You need friends."

"No, I don't."

Brown eyes narrowed but Roxie held Lauren's gaze. If the busybody wanted a staring contest, Lauren would oblige. Seconds passed with neither blinking, until Roxie broke first.

"You're stubborn. I like that. We're going to get along, you and me." Before Lauren could process that statement, Roxie leaned forward and rested her elbows on the desk. "Now, about Will. There are three things you need to know about our boss. One, she's the most generous person you'll ever meet. Two, she also works harder than anyone in the history of ever. And three, she's like the unofficial mayor of Anchor Island. She and Randy own five businesses here, and everything they do is for the betterment of both the islanders and the island."

Unsure how to respond, Lauren once again chose silence, which she assumed Roxie would fill. She was right.

"Despite her busy schedule, much of what Will does is volunteer work, and the festival committee, which organizes all island activities, is something she'd never give up."

Pointing out what felt like the obvious, Lauren said, "If it's a committee, then there must be plenty of other people to handle her stepping away for one time from one event. I'm not asking her to take a vacation or to stop volunteering. I'm simply asking her to put the restaurant first. How am I supposed to stand on the sidelines while every chef on the coast competes for best food?"

Roxie leaned back again. "When you put it that way, it does sound a bit more reasonable. But it also sounds like you want her to put you first more than the restaurant."

Lauren rose from her chair. "I *am* the restaurant. My success is Pilar's success. That in turn becomes

Will's success. Isn't that the point of running a business?"

The wide grin curled Roxie's glossy lips. "You aren't good at compromise, are you?"

"No."

"That must make life pretty complicated at times."

"Yes," Lauren replied. More than complicated, but she would not apologize for who she was.

With a nod, the other woman rose. "Then I'll talk to her."

"You will?"

"I'm happy to go to bat for a friend."

"But we aren't—"

"Sure we are," Roxie cut in. "You'll get used to it."

For her own comfort, Lauren changed the word friend to ally in her mind, and those she could use.

"Let me know what she says."

As Lauren headed for the door, Roxie added, "I expect a free meal as payment."

"That I can do."

———

"You've got a visitor," Annie Littleton, a long time Dempsey's waitress, called into the kitchen.

"Who is it?" he asked, continuing to break down the chicken on his cutting board.

"Jackson Moore."

A native islander who had been Nick's equal at the

Marina restaurant before the Navarros bought it, Jackson had become a good friend within weeks of Nick moving to the island. They'd talked shop, women, and sports, in that order.

"Tell him I'll be right out." Pulling off his latex gloves, Nick called out to Carl who was exiting the cooler. "Take over here, will you?"

"Sure thing, boss."

Nick washed his hands, then crossed through the kitchen while drying them. As he stepped out behind the bar, he tossed the towel over his left shoulder. "Hey, man. What's up?"

Jackson's typical easy smile was nowhere to be seen. "Can we talk?"

"Yeah, I've got a few minutes."

When Nick remained behind the counter, the older man nodded toward a table by the windows. "Over there?"

"Sure. Let me come around." Nick went back through the kitchen and exited the side door close to the table where Jackson had taken a seat. "Is Denise okay?" he asked, concerned something had happened to Jackson's wife.

Dark wrinkles covered the man's forehead as the sun glistened off his bald black head. "She's good. Ornery as ever, but good. I'm here about that new chef."

"What about her?"

"I got an email about interviews for the new

restaurant. The chef has some requirements for anyone looking to apply. High requirements."

Nick had been afraid of this. "What are they?"

Jackson rubbed his burn-scarred hands together. "A minimum of five years' experience for all positions from cooks on down."

"Shit," Nick mumbled, running a hand through his hair. That would cut nearly everyone out. "What else?"

"For cooks, we have to have worked in at least three different restaurants, and fast food doesn't count. Neither do diners."

That put Jackson out as well.

"Where does she think she's going to find these people?" he asked.

"Hell if I know." Jackson straightened and crossed his arms as his dark gaze shifted toward the scene outside the window. "Since they closed down for the remodel, I've picked up some work here and there, but I was counting on getting that job back." His eyes cut to Nick, worry clear in their brown depths. "We can't live on what Denise makes at the school alone. If I can't get back on, we'll have to think about moving off the island."

This was a reality that every local faced eventually. In a village only a square mile wide, job opportunities were slim, which was the reason efforts to boost tourism had been rampant in the last ten years, and why hiring islanders had been a priority for all local businesses.

There were commuters who came in from Hatteras, but those were the exception not the rule.

"Once she learns how long you were there, she has to give you a chance." Jackson had worked in that kitchen for fifteen years. He knew how to keep the line going, handle unhappy customers, and could work every station from sauces to expediting. She'd be an idiot not to bring him back.

He shook his head. "I don't know, man. It isn't looking good."

Unwilling to let his friend suffer, Nick said, "I'll talk to her."

Jackson's eyes went wide. "You know her?"

"I've met her," Nick explained. "Mia did some work in the dining room last week and I was there to see it. The woman's a hard-ass, like every other ambitious chef, but she's going to need good people. If she isn't willing to bend on this experience bullshit, she'll be running that kitchen by herself."

"Mona and Deborah are the only two who meet the requirements," his friend pointed out. "I have to wonder if their personalities are going to mix with hers."

Like Nick, Mona Bradwell had spent years in restaurant kitchens from Charlotte to Raleigh to Atlantic City. Along the way she'd developed a resistance to hotheaded chefs. Jackson was as calm and fair as he was kind, and after six months in his kitchen, Mona had declared that she'd never work for anyone else.

Deborah Prince had arrived on the island around the same time as Nick. Like Chef Riley, she was classically trained but in pastry instead of straight culinary. That didn't mean she couldn't hold her own at any station. Where Mona enjoyed being on the line and managing the chaos, Deborah preferred to be left to her own duties, away from the others and out of the noise.

Nick had no idea how Lauren Riley would run her kitchen. She didn't seem like the type to scream and curse through a service, but he didn't see her as the nurturing type either. If she planned to hold her staff to Boston fine-dining standards, then she'd better be ready for some serious turnover. Or have a lot of friends willing to come work on a remote, Outer Banks Island.

"Have you talked to either of them?" he asked.

"Not since getting the email, but a week ago they both intended to go back. They also assumed I'd be there, so their intentions might be different now."

Nick bolted to his feet. "You'll be there. I'll see to it."

No doubt the woman would balk at his interference, but someone had to talk some sense into her.

"I appreciate anything you can do," Jackson said as he rose more slowly to his feet. "I haven't told Denise about the email yet. I don't want her to worry."

"We'll get it worked out." The two exchanged a handshake and Jackson tapped Nick on the shoulder.

"I hope you're right. I'll owe you big-time if you can change her mind."

"Keep me stocked in Denise's clam chowder and

we'll be good." The woman refused to tell Nick her secret recipe and all his attempts to replicate the flavors had failed.

"You've got it." Stepping back, Jackson said, "See you, Annie," to the waitress at the end of the bar.

"Bye, Jack." As Nick passed on his way to the kitchen, she asked, "Is everything okay? He didn't look like his normal happy self."

Nick didn't feel it was right to share his friend's private business. "He's fine. Just a little problem I said I'd help him with."

"Can I do anything?"

When he'd first come to Anchor, Nick had taken the islanders' constant offers of assistance as small-town folks butting into their neighbor's business. He knew better now. Whether from forced proximity or shared experiences due to the often turbulent weather that came with living on a barrier island, the locals here operated more like a family than a bunch of individuals who happened to share a zip code.

There was dysfunction at times, like with any family, but they had each other's backs when it counted, and if helping Jackson required going toe to toe with Lauren Riley, then Nick was more than willing to do so.

"I've got this," he said, "but thanks for the offer."

———

LAUREN PRESSED the button on the measuring tape and it snapped back into place. This time she managed not to pinch her finger.

"I could put two tables that way, or three tables this way." She turned with arms extended, trying to imagine the setup. "But this way there wouldn't be enough room for the servers."

Teeth clenched on the tip of her thumbnail, she spun again, trying to see the area from multiple angles. Both the number of seats and the configuration of the dining room were crucial components to a successful restaurant. Tables could be moved, of course, should the original layout prove too cumbersome—or the opposite, far too spread out—but Lauren liked to get things right the first time.

"I wish we could get rid of this half wall," she mumbled.

"Who are you talking to?"

Lauren jumped at the unexpected question, dropping the measuring tape on her big toe.

"Son of a bitch," she growled, bending over and grabbing her injured digit. Jumping around on one foot, she shot Nick an angry scowl. "What are you doing here?"

"I came to talk to you," he said, sliding a leather jacket down his arms and draping it over the hostess stand. "Are you okay?"

She set her foot back on the floor and straightened.

"I'm fine. Who said you could come in? We aren't open yet."

Nick glanced around the empty dining room. "Really? I'd never have known."

Strolling across the restaurant, he came to a stop closer than Lauren was comfortable with, but stepping back would be a sign of weakness. She'd learned long ago how men treated a weak woman.

"If you want to keep people out, then you should lock the door. We need to talk about these requirements for your staff."

"How would you know what my requirements are?" she asked, using the excuse of picking up the tape measure to put distance between them.

"It's a small island. People talk."

Of course they did.

"Are you looking to apply?" she asked, maintaining a neutral expression while her body tightened at the idea.

Not that she was afraid of him, exactly. There was just something about him. An air of confidence and the look of a man used to being in control. Lauren knew herself well enough to know she lacked the grit required to stand up to him in the kitchen. At least she did right now. Once Pilar's was launched and successful, she'd be more confident.

"You'd be lucky if I did, but no. This insistence that cooks have experience in multiple restaurants is never going to work."

Refusing to let him rile her, she kept her voice level. "Says who?"

"Says reality. In case you haven't noticed, you're on an island. A small one. There are plenty of people here who can handle whatever you need in that kitchen, but you have to be willing to give them a chance."

"Last I checked, I'm the person opening this restaurant, not you. Pilar's is not going to be a bar and grill. We'll be serving more elevated food." Lauren pointed at him with the tape measure. "So you stick to what you do, and I'll do what I do, and we'll stay out of each other's way."

Finished talking, she marched off toward the kitchen, but Nick's next words stopped her cold.

"You're messing with people's lives." When Lauren turned around, he continued. "I told you before. We take care of our own. Jobs aren't overflowing in a place like this. Jackson Moore ran that kitchen long before you ever touched a knife. Dismissing fifteen years on the front line because it all happened in one place isn't just shortsighted, it's mean."

She'd had no idea how long the previous staff had worked at the restaurant, nor had she done her homework to find out. A confession she kept to herself.

"Are you finished?"

"Are you going to give these people a chance?"

Nodding toward the door, she said, "I have a dining room to design. You saw yourself in. You can see yourself out."

His jaw twitched but he swallowed whatever argument would come next and stormed over to his jacket. As he shoved his arm in the sleeve, Nick offered one last parting shot.

"Maybe you've never struggled to make ends meet, but life is different here. If there's an ounce of compassion in that cold heart of yours, consider what you're doing. Otherwise, you'll be running that kitchen all by yourself."

He was wrong about one thing. Lauren knew struggle better than most. But he'd gotten the cold heart right. That heart protected her. Kept her safe. If this Jackson Moore person knew his way around the kitchen, as Nick claimed, then she *would* give him a chance. Not because Nick Stamatis had demanded she do so, but because she wanted experienced people on her team.

Leaving the tape measure on the pass, she turned toward her office, knowing exactly who to call for details on the previous staff. Roxie would likely require a second meal as payment, but at least Lauren would have someone to try her new dishes on.

3

IN THE TWO DAYS SINCE HE'D PAID CHEF RILEY A VISIT, Nick hadn't been able to get her out of his head. She hadn't known about Jackson. She hadn't known about any of the people who had worked in that restaurant before she took over. Proof that she'd never run a damn kitchen before.

That would have been his first question if he'd been offered a job like that. *Who do I have to work with?* Yet the thing he really couldn't get out of his head was the fear in her eyes. She hid it well. That icy facade covered a lot, but that facade had slipped for mere seconds and the truth had shown through.

Lauren Riley was in over her head.

Nick had never been the stalker type, but doing an internet search on a fellow chef wasn't the same as digging up dirt on an ex. The few facts he had going in—

hometown Boston, attended Le Cordon Bleu—were enough to narrow down the search. The lack of info available confirmed his suspicions. She'd never run a kitchen before. As far as he could tell, she'd never even been second-in-command. Or third.

What had possessed Will Navarro to hand her this restaurant?

Hopefully, she'd worked under some quality leaders, but based on her current methodology for picking staff, he had to wonder.

"Just the man I came to see," Jackson called out as he crossed the restaurant toward the bar where Nick was taking a break. The big man set a sealed plastic container on the counter. "I'm here to pay up."

Unsure what he'd done, Nick examined the bowl. "Pay up for what?"

"You did it, man. I got the email this morning. The new chef is giving me an interview."

Not what he'd expected. "That's good. I'm glad she came around."

"Doesn't mean I'll get my job back, but at least I'm in the running." Jackson tapped the lid of the container. "Denise's clam chowder, as promised. I'll bring another helping next week."

Rising up on his stool, Nick reached over the bar and snagged a spoon. "The perfect meal on a chilly April day." The first bite was heaven. The second even better. Cooking was all about flavor and balance, and Denise somehow managed to add the perfect amount of acidity without throwing off the taste. "How much vinegar does she put in here?"

Jackson laughed. "You know I can't tell you that. Besides, I'm not sure I know myself. She keeps this recipe under lock and key and won't let me anywhere near the kitchen while she makes it. She says what makes it so good is in the cook, not the cooking, and since I have to live with her, I'm not going to argue."

Nick wasn't going to argue with her either. There were mystical elements at play in the making of amazing food, and whatever powers his friend's wife possessed, he was just grateful that she used them for his benefit.

While enjoying the chowder, Nick asked, "What exactly did the email say?" Lauren's parting shot about running things her own way had not seemed like a concession to his demands.

"That due to my long history with the restaurant, I was being invited to interview. I don't know what you said, but it worked."

Maybe she was willing to listen after all. "I only pointed out that she was going to miss out on some great cooks. Did anyone else get the invite?"

"The whole staff, as far as I know. We could have the team back together in no time."

Good news, but a development that would leave Lauren as the sole outsider. Another hurdle she likely wasn't equipped to clear.

"That's good. I'm glad I could help." From the corner

of his eye, Nick saw two women enter the restaurant. "Speak of the devil. Here's the new chef now."

Lauren and Roxie Chandler lingered by the door, and after a brief exchange, Roxie shuffled off toward the restrooms. Lauren looked around and eventually caught Nick's gaze. He nodded in greeting, and she visibly tensed. A second before she'd looked like a kid walking into a new school for the first time. After seeing Nick, she looked more like a dragon ready for battle.

"Should I introduce myself?" Jackson asked.

Curious how she'd respond, Nick slid off his stool. "Definitely. Let's go."

The two men crossed to the entrance and Lauren's body language gave off a fight or flight vibe as they did so. Sensing her unease, Nick stopped several feet away.

"Chef Riley, this is Jackson Moore. I'm guessing you recognize the name."

Blue eyes shifted to his friend and her face softened. "Nice to meet you, Mr. Moore."

"Call me Jackson," he said. "I appreciate the opportunity to interview for the new restaurant."

"After fifteen years of service, you've more than earned the right."

"Thank you, Chef. I'll see you tomorrow, then."

Lauren smiled, cracking the icy shell to which Nick had grown accustomed. "I'm looking forward to it."

Jackson bid Nick farewell and left the restaurant, leaving him alone with Lauren.

"Thank you," he said.

The cold front returned. "For what?" she asked, avoiding eye contact.

"You know what."

She lifted her chin and met his gaze. "I didn't give him an interview because of you. As I told you once, I never said I wouldn't hire locals. That was your assumption."

"So you planned to offer them all interviews from the beginning?"

The flinch was telling. "They were with the restaurant long enough to earn at least that. Just like I told Jackson."

Not an answer to his question, but Nick let her slide. "Either way, thanks for giving them a chance."

"I'm back," Roxie said as she joined them. "Hey, Nick. How's it going?"

"It's good, Roxie. You ladies need a table?"

"We're waiting for the others, but we could sit and wait. Table for seven."

He turned back to the bar. "Georgette, bring seven menus over to table nine."

"On my way," the waitress replied as Nick led the customers to a large round booth in the center of the room. "Here you go. Georgette will take care of you."

"Thanks," Roxie said, plopping onto the red vinyl seat as Lauren sat down on the opposite side.

Before leaving them, Nick bent to whisper something only she could hear. "I'm around if you have any questions."

Lauren scooted farther into the booth. "Thanks, but no thanks."

He'd extended the branch. That was all he could do.

Georgette arrived and spread the menus around the table. "Can I get you ladies some drinks or do you want to wait?"

"I'll take an iced tea," Roxie replied, flipping a menu open.

"Okay, and you, hun?" she said to Lauren, who ignored the menu in front of her.

"Water, please."

"Yes, ma'am."

Nick left the table with Georgette and once they were far enough away, the waitress whispered, "Isn't that the new chef Will hired?"

"That's her."

"She seems so meek," the waitress observed.

"She isn't," Nick said.

Georgette scoffed. "If you say so."

They parted ways at the bar and Nick took a left toward the entrance to the kitchen. In the doorway, he glanced back to find Roxie talking up a storm and Lauren nodding along silently. As if sensing his gaze, her eyes cut his way. He couldn't read her expression, but he got the sense she was asking for something. What, he didn't know. His help? His silence? His early demise?

She looked away first and Nick stepped into the kitchen with one thought in mind. If she went down, so did Will and Randy, and whatever kitchen crew she brought on board. He'd be an ass to let that happen when he could do something about it.

Lauren Riley may not want his help, but she sure as hell needed it. For her sake, and for everyone else's.

———

"You don't need to worry about Nick," Roxie said, causing Lauren to nearly stick the paper straw up her nose.

She lowered her water glass back to the table. "Excuse me?"

"He hits on everyone."

"He does what?"

Roxie shook her head. "He hits on every woman he meets. It's his thing." When Lauren stared blankly, she added, "Unless you're interested. I mean, I wouldn't blame you. He's gorgeous as hell and that bad boy vibe is tough for any red-blooded female to resist. If I hadn't broken that habit when meeting Alex, I might have taken a ride on the Nick train myself, but I'm immune to him now."

Lauren felt as if she were the one taking a ride. "I'm sorry. What are you talking about?"

Heavily lashed brown eyes cut to the bar and back. "Whatever he just whispered in your ear."

"That wasn't—"

"You don't have to tell me what he said." She focused

on her menu. "I mean, I can imagine. If you're game, then I say go for it."

"Who's going for what?" Will asked as she scooted into the booth opposite Lauren.

"The newbie is into Nick."

"Really?" said a woman with a head full of curly hair.

"No, I—"

"Don't forget the parachute," muttered a tiny woman wearing oversized clothes who was quite possibly the most beautiful human Lauren had ever seen. She dropped down onto the seat and forced Lauren to scoot in. "That man has got to be carrying something."

"That's mean," scolded the blonde who slid in next. "Nick is a nice guy. Mia says he doesn't deserve that reputation."

Another blonde who looked very similar to the first sat down on the other side of the table. "She's his sister. She has to say that."

Squeezed in next to Roxie, Lauren felt both overwhelmed and claustrophobic. When invited to a Sunday brunch with *the girls,* she'd accepted only because Roxie had refused to take no for an answer. She'd even tried backing out once learning the location, but the bossy brunette wouldn't hear of it.

"You're scaring our new friend," Roxie said, silencing the chatter. "Time for introductions. You know Will," she said, starting on her right. "Then we have Beth Chandler, my cousin and the nicest person you'll ever meet. Next to her is Henri Bloom, who writes steamy books and is Callie's cousin." A slender black-tipped finger pointed to the person two down from Lauren. "That's Callie Edwards, mother of three, including brand-new twins, and a total super woman. Sid is the one next to you," she finished.

"Are you not going to say anything else about Sid?" Beth asked.

"Relax, curly," the woman in question mumbled into her menu. "Rox is still pissed that my truck is faster than her car."

"I had to slow down to avoid the cat," Roxie argued.

"You shouldn't have been racing in the first place," Will pointed out.

"Weren't we talking about Nick?" Sid said, reaching for the bucket of peanuts in the center of the table. When her arm proved too short to touch the rim, Callie moved the bucket closer. "Thanks," the smaller woman said.

"He *is* attractive," Beth pointed out. "Joe says he's against commitment, though, so I'd be careful if you're looking for more than a good time."

All eyes turned to Lauren, who took several seconds to realize they were waiting for her to weigh in. "I'm not looking for anything. From Nick or anyone else." A collective groan echoed around the table. "Did I say something wrong?"

Henri chuckled. "These ladies are all married and were hoping to live vicariously through you."

"I'm not married," Roxie corrected.

"You might as well be," Beth said. "It's nice to meet you, Lauren. Welcome to Anchor Island."

"Um...thanks."

Georgette returned to the table to take the newcomers' drink orders, and everyone gave their food order as well since they were familiar with the menu. Lauren was not and quickly scanned the options. The offerings were dominated by seafood, as expected. They *were* on an island, after all. Her turn came before she'd skimmed to the end so she went with the last item she read.

"I'll have the crab cake, please."

"Entree or sandwich," the waitress asked.

"Sandwich."

"A side?"

Lauren quickly found that section. "Hush puppies is fine."

"You've got it."

As the server moved on to Sid, Lauren took a moment to take in her surroundings. Dempsey's was not lacking in color, despite every surface, from tables to chairs to floor and ceiling, being made of polished wood. Neon lights and various alcohol brand advertisements dotted the walls in what she could only describe as organized chaos. License plates from all over the country lined the beams that ran from front to back the length of the room.

The place was homey, welcoming, broken in, and full

of character. Lauren's penchant for fine dining did not make her immune to the rustic charm of the place. She'd never worked in a sports bar, but plenty of small family-owned establishments could take up space on her resume if she ever decided to include every job she ever had, which would require multiple pages.

The longest she'd worked in one place was thirteen months. Lauren had never been outright fired. Either her fellow cooks had made her life a living hell until she could no longer tolerate the stress, or her employer had cut her hours to the point she could no longer make a living.

Though Lauren had made no real attempts to fit in, she'd also not gone out of her way to alienate people. That skill just came naturally. Lucky for her.

"Where are you from originally, Lauren?" Beth asked, drawing her attention back to the table.

"Boston," she replied.

"Will's from Boston," Sid pointed out. "Did your families know each other?"

Lauren wasn't aware they'd come from the same town. "I'm not sure. What area are you from?" she asked her boss.

"We moved around quite a bit when I was young, but my mother's family is from Back Bay-Beacon Hill."

Lauren was glad she didn't have a drink in her hand. She'd likely have dropped it in her lap or done a spit-take across the table. Back Bay-Beacon Hill was the wealthiest neighborhood in Boston, which was already one of the richest cities in the country. Lauren's life in Worcester had been one of poverty, not wealth.

Rationally, Lauren knew that growing up poor did not define her, nor did it make her inferior to any of the women at the table. Yet deep-seated insecurities had a way of making a person feel small no matter how hard they fought to suppress them.

"Then no," she said, dropping her gaze. "I'm sure our paths never crossed."

"It's a big city so that's not surprising," Beth offered. "I almost moved there once. I was all packed to go, but then Joe showed up at my door and I guess the rest is history."

"Come on, curly. Tell her how you and Joe met," Sid said before yipping in pain. "What the—"

"How are the twins, Callie?" Will asked, changing the subject and leaving Lauren curious about Beth's story.

"Exhausting," the new mother replied. "This is my first week back to work and though it's only for a few hours a day, I hate being away from them."

"You get used to it," Sid assured her. "Lucas had a terrible time leaving Pilar for even an hour in that first year, but she's so happy at the daycare that now it's totally natural."

"Pilar?" Lauren repeated. "Like the restaurant?"

"Sid is Randy's sister," Will explained, "and Pilar was their mother's name. We named the restaurant after her."

"Don't try to tell my child that," Sid said. "When she

saw the new sign the other day, she couldn't stop talking about how Uncle Randy named his 'restant' after her."

"Then we won't tell her otherwise," Will said with a laugh.

"Here we go, ladies," their waitress said, returning with a large tray on her shoulder. With practiced ease, she slid it onto the empty table next door and started passing out the dishes. Once everyone had their meals, the chatter ebbed to quiet conversations between neighbors. With the odd number, that left Lauren eating in silence.

Halfway through what she had to reluctantly admit was an impressively delicious crab cake, Roxie bumped her shoulder.

"You okay?" she asked.

Mouth full, Lauren nodded.

"They're a lot," Roxie whispered, "but they're really cool."

Having no grounds to argue, Lauren nodded again and Roxie returned to her conversation with Will. Taking another bite of her crab cake, she couldn't help but sigh with pleasure. The texture was perfect. The acidity just right. Glancing toward the bar, she caught Nick watching her through the window to the kitchen. A dark brow arched in silent question, and she raised her fork in an approving salute.

The smile that split his face threatened to stop her heart, and a second later he disappeared from the window. Her mind raced back to something Roxie had said before the others arrived.

He hits on everyone.

Well, not *everyone*.

4

BELIEVING THE END OF HIS LIFE WAS NEAR DID NOT MEAN Nick would help move things along. He'd been eating clean since his mid-twenties, and thanks to the island farmer's market, he was able to find fresh fruits and vegetables throughout the year. Farmers, along with weekend gardeners, made the trip from the mainland once a month in the winter and twice a month from spring to fall. Nick shaped his diet around whatever was in season, which in April included beets, leeks, chard, and fennel with a dash of arugula and cilantro thrown in.

Strawberries would arrive soon, which meant his smoothies would improve considerably. Greens were good, but even better with fruit in the mix.

Nick examined a bushel of collard greens. "Looking good today, Cai. I'll take these." He handed over four bunches of the leafy greens.

"You've got it, Mr. Nick." The farmer slid the vegetables into a small brown bag and snapped a rubber band around the middle. Originally from China, Cai Qian knew every customer on the island by name and never failed to greet them with a smile. He also traveled the farthest distance to reach the market, but kept his prices competitive with the other vendors despite the added overhead.

"How is the summer squash looking?" Nick asked. "Do you think you'll have some available next month?"

"Yes, sir. The squash is looking beautiful." After handing over the greens, he gave a thumbs-up. "Almost ready."

Making his baked Parmesan coated squash rounds always signaled the beginning of summer for Nick. "Looking forward to them."

Tucking his change into his pocket, Nick turned to leave, only to collide with another shopper. The collard greens hit the floor as he reached out to steady the person and found his hands wrapped around Lauren Riley's waist. They stared at each other in shock for several seconds before she jerked back, forcing him to let go.

The warmth of her body continued to resonate against his palms.

"I'm sorry I—" she started.

"I didn't—" Nick said at the same time.

"...see you," they both finished.

"Are you okay?" he asked. He'd hit her pretty hard

and though Lauren was tall, she was slender. "Did I hurt you?"

She shook her head and tucked a platinum lock behind her ear. "No. I'm fine. I should have been paying more attention."

"No, I should have looked before I turned."

Feeling like a preteen who'd brushed against a girl for the first time, Nick bent to pick up his greens. Lauren did the same and they collided again, this time with their foreheads. He jerked back up to find her holding her head and, to his surprise, she was laughing.

"I didn't think you did that," he said, bending to retrieve the greens.

"Do what?" Lauren asked.

"Laugh."

She sobered and light brows drew together. "I'm not a robot."

He remembered the feel of her in his hands and had to agree. "It's nice."

"What is?"

"Your laugh."

Crossing her arms, she tapped a finger on her elbow. "Are you finally hitting on me?"

The finally threw him off. "Excuse me?"

"Roxie said you hit on everyone, but you haven't hit on me."

Until this moment, he'd never regretted the reputation he'd carefully cultivated since arriving on the island.

"You and Roxie are both wrong. I don't hit on everyone, and I'm not hitting on you."

Lauren straightened. "Why not?"

"Why not what?"

"Why aren't you hitting on me? What's wrong with me?"

If she was trying to confuse him, she was doing a bang-up job. "You *want* me to hit on you?"

"I didn't say that."

"I think you did."

She huffed as if he was the one being difficult. "I'm just curious, that's all. If someone said you give candy bars to everyone but you didn't give one to me, I'd be asking the same question."

To appease her curiosity, Nick said, "You're a chef."

"What does that have to do with anything?"

"I don't hit on chefs."

Holding his gaze, she looked to be assessing the truthfulness of his answer. "So if I wasn't a chef, you'd hit on me?"

If he said yes, he was the horndog Roxie had made him out to be. If he said no, he'd be lying.

"Is this your way of hitting *on me*?" he asked.

Lauren bristled. "I am *not* hitting on you."

"But you want to."

During their previous encounters, she'd been an expert at hiding her thoughts, so watching her struggle to maintain that cool demeanor through this conversation was highly entertaining.

"To be clear," she said, "I am *not* hitting on you. I do not *want* to hit on you. And I don't want *you* to hit on *me*." The icy glare returned. "Now if you'll excuse me."

"I could show you around," Nick said. The words were out of his mouth before he knew what he was saying.

She met his eyes and he could see the tension in their blue depths. "Around what?"

"The market." Nick waved to encompass their surroundings. "Some of these vendors offer larger shipments for the restaurants. You'll need the connections, and this would give you a good opportunity to find out what's available to build out your menu."

Indecision softened her features as she glanced around. "I would like to line up some suppliers."

"Then now's your chance. Follow me."

Nick led her down the center aisle and around to the larger stands outside the pavilion. Knowing that proteins would be her most important ingredients, he headed straight for Martha Dowry's stand.

"Hey, Martha. I have a new customer for you."

The older woman looked up over the rim of the small round reading glasses that were ever-present on the tip of her nose. Sharp green eyes locked on Lauren. "I've never seen you around before."

"I'm new," Lauren replied.

"From where?" Martha asked.

"Boston."

With a huff of derision, Martha crossed her arms. "What can I do for you?"

Nick made the introductions. "This is Lauren Riley. She's the new chef over at the old Marina restaurant."

"It's called Pilar's now," Lauren added.

Thin lips settled into a hard line. "What kind of food do you plan to make?"

"Sophisticated fare that offers visitors to the island something more discriminating than what they can get right now."

Both brows shot up as Martha shifted her gaze to Nick. "More discriminating? She hasn't been here long, has she?"

"A little over two weeks," she answered for herself. "I'm sure there are tourists who would appreciate a dining option a level above what's already available."

The two women embarked on a staring contest and Nick was smart enough to keep his mouth shut. Martha was old school. She didn't like city folk, as she called them, nor was she the fine dining type. But she did admire grit and a strong work ethic. Both of which Nick had no doubt Lauren possessed.

"What's your best dish?" Martha asked, breaking the silence.

"I don't have only one best dish, but a favorite is cock crab and poached lobster with a bouillabaisse sauce."

Not a surprise coming from a New England chef.

"I prefer scallops," Martha replied.

"Then you'll have to come in for my Dived scallops

with charred leeks in an onion broth. Provided I can find a supplier for them." The display between the two women was covered in various seafood options, and Lauren's eyes cut to the scallops on the right. "These look good."

As if signaling the end of the battle, the older woman grinned. "I've got the best scallops from Norfolk to Hilton Head. Buy from me and you'll be set."

"Do you have a business card?" Lauren asked.

"I can do you one better." Martha bent over, disappearing behind the stand, and then popped back up a second later. "A magnet." She handed Lauren a bright red, crab-shaped item. "Stick that on your fridge or file cabinet so you'll always know where to find me."

The corner of Lauren's mouth lifted as she accepted the magnet. "I'll be sure to do that."

The pair said their goodbyes and moved on, with Martha yelling, "Call me!" as they left.

"Is everyone a character around here?" Lauren asked, eyes on the magnetic crustacean in her hand.

"Pretty much, but you get used to them." A passerby carrying four loaded bags of vegetables veered close, forcing Nick to pull Lauren out of the way. "You need to watch where you're going."

She shook her head as if returning to the present. "Sorry. This just reminded me of when I was a kid. We had something similar on our refrigerators."

"Refrigerators? Plural?"

"We moved a lot." Tucking the magnet into the back

pocket of her jeans, she added, "The magnets changed fridges a lot."

"To different towns?"

"No." The smile didn't reach her eyes. "Just around Worcester. Who do we see next?"

Nick glanced down the aisle. "Trenton works for a local fisherman out of Hatteras and is a good option for fresh crab."

Lauren leveled a hand across her brows to block out the sun. "Then I definitely need to meet him."

"Last stand on the right." He extended a hand for her to go first. "I'll follow behind to make sure you don't have any more near-accidents."

She rolled her eyes but didn't argue, and Nick fell into step behind her, curious why a family would move around in the same town. The only two reasons he could think of were to improve their situation or because they didn't have a choice. Either way, spending your childhood constantly having to adapt to new situations couldn't have been fun, and might explain the wall of ice she kept between herself and everyone else.

That wall could protect, but it could also make life pretty damn lonely. Something Nick knew all too well.

———

NICK STAMATIS WAS easy to be with and smelled like a mix of patchouli, sandalwood, and vanilla all rolled into one. A heady scent that threatened to make her forget he wasn't her favorite person.

His generous, no-pretense attitude also disarmed her. Not counting their hit-on-or-not-hit-on conversation, they'd spent a comfortable hour together exploring the farmer's market. He spoke to her as a peer, which was novel in her experience, but at the same time he'd educated her on the ins and outs of finding food suppliers on an island as remote as Anchor.

When she'd accepted the job at Pilar's, that had been Lauren's biggest concern. *Could she get the ingredients she needed to make her dishes sing?* Thanks to Nick, she now had a pocket full of business cards plus one crab-shaped magnet that would help her keep the pantry stocked.

"Have you come up with a menu yet?" Nick asked as they rested at a picnic table with two peach iced teas they'd purchased from a food truck.

"I have a few staples I know I want to add, but now there are all sorts of ideas racing through my head." She'd known an island would rely heavily on seafood, but she was surprised by the other proteins that were available. All fresh and naturally sourced.

"How about items from the Marina menu? Are you considering any of those?"

Lauren hadn't planned on incorporating any dishes from the previous restaurant. "Not really. I'd rather create my own."

Nick rubbed a thumb down the side of his paper cup. "You aren't just feeding the tourists. You're feeding the locals, too. The Marina operated for thirty-two years for a reason. It couldn't hurt to pick one or two favorites to make the place feel familiar."

Something to consider. If she hired any of the previous staff, she'd take suggestions from them and have them prepare the dishes she believed might fit her concept. After tasting the options she'd make a final decision.

"Did you apply for this job?" she asked, truly curious.

"What job?"

"My job," she clarified. "You seem to have put a lot of thought into how to get Pilar's up and running. Odd for a man who has his own kitchen to think about."

Nick shook his head with a chuckle. "No, I didn't apply. I'm just thinking about what's best for this island and the people on it. It's a habit. Once you're here for a while, you'll do the same."

Would she? Lauren had never been a joiner or put much thought into the community around her. All of her past experience was in urban areas where people minded their own business and preferred that others do the same. Plus, the demands of restaurant work barely left time for sleep let alone neighborly concern.

Changing the subject, she asked, "How does the Best of the Fest contest work?"

Nick rolled with the change. "Food is served throughout the three-day event and on Sunday, attendees cast their votes for one final dish that each vendor puts forward."

Lauren sat up straighter. "So the committee doesn't pick the winner?"

"No," Nick replied, shaking his head, "but they have to count the votes. That's where your conflict of interest comes in."

"I still don't see the problem." She finished the last of her tea and rose to her feet. "Are there categories or does everyone compete against each other across the board?"

Nick finished his own drink and followed her lead, retrieving his bag of vegetables off the bench beside him. They tossed their cups in the green recycle can as he said, "There are things like best burger and best seafood dish, but the Best of the Fest is an overall award."

"What dish did you win with the last two years?" Lauren asked as they strolled side by side back to the main market area.

"The first year was my lobster linguine with chiles," Nick said, "and then last year I made an artichoke chowder with soft-shell clams."

Lauren stopped walking. "But Dempsey's menu is all bar food."

Two steps ahead of her, Nick stopped and turned around. "Yeah, but that isn't all that I make."

"If you can make dishes like that, then why do you work at a bar?"

His eyes turned dark as his jaw tightened. "Cooking

is cooking. So long as it's full of flavor and satisfying, then no one food is better than another."

She begged to differ. "Bullshit."

"Not bullshit."

"The hell it isn't. There's a reason a burger joint has never won a Michelin star."

"And plenty of Michelin star restaurants have burgers on their menus. It isn't what you make, Lauren. It's how you make it." Shaking his head, he added, "Any chef worthy of the title should know that."

Fuck that.

"Last I checked, you were a head cook without a culinary education. You can tell yourself learning on the line is the same, but it isn't. So the next time you feel like handing out free advice, save us both the time and stick it up your ass."

Pulling her keys from her pocket, Lauren strode off toward the parking area and could almost feel the smoke coming out of her ears. She *was* a chef, goddamn it, and she didn't need Nick Stamatis or anyone else's approval to claim the title. *Not about what you make?* What nonsense. A chef's dishes were an extension of who they were. The culmination of years spent mastering techniques and honing their skills to be the best.

Lauren *would be* considered one of the best someday. Even if it was over one bar cook's dead body.

———

"WHAT THE HELL did you say to her?"

Nick spun to find Mona Bradwell behind him, her eyes on Lauren in the distance. A ball cap covered her short black hair and a pair of sunglasses sat atop the bill of the hat. The UNC hoodie was two sizes too big for her, but matched the teal Chucks.

"Something she didn't want to hear," he replied. "That's what you get to deal with if you go back."

Mona smiled. "The only part I heard was her telling you to shove it up your ass. I like her."

Not the reaction he expected. "I thought you didn't like hotheaded chefs."

"Who says she's hotheaded?"

He looked toward Lauren and back. "Did you not just see that?"

The woman share a wry smile. "You pissed her off and she snapped back. That makes her ballsy in my book. Let me guess. You were telling her how to run her restaurant."

Not exactly. At least not in that moment.

"All I did was point out that fine dining isn't superior to bar food." And he'd questioned her right to call herself a chef, which had been out of line.

"According to whom?" Mona shook her head. "Nobody is going to pay caviar prices for one of your crab cakes."

"Who's selling caviar?" Deborah Prince asked as she joined them. He should have known the two would be together. Deborah's sweatshirt was similar to Mona's, as they both had daughters who attended the university.

Mona turned to face her friend. "Mr. Nick here thinks his bar fare is on the fine dining level."

"I never said that."

"The male ego is a wondrous thing," Deborah said, ignoring his response. "I can't argue that Dempsey's serves good food, but you are not serving up anything that competes with a five-star restaurant."

"I didn't say Dempsey's is a five-star restaurant."

"You said it was just as good."

"I'm saying all food is equal so long as it makes people happy."

Deborah snorted. "My husband makes me happy, but I don't delude myself into thinking he's just as good as George Clooney."

"George is so fine," Mona mumbled.

"Yes, he is."

Nick was losing control of this conversation. "Who said anything about George Clooney?"

"It's called an analogy," Deborah replied. "Proof that all men are not created equal, just like all food is not created equal. What's good will always be subjective, but equal is a whole other matter."

"The best cheeseburger is never going to beat the best filet mignon," Mona added. "So I see why Chef Riley told you to stick it up your ass."

"She said that?" Deborah asked.

"Loud and clear," Mona assured her.

"Then I like her already."

This was not how Nick saw his morning going. "We'll see if you two feel the same after spending a week in her kitchen. And that's *if* she gives you a job."

"I sense a little rivalry going on," Mona murmured.

"He's definitely feeling threatened," Deborah nodded.

Nick didn't like that implication. "I am *not* threatened by Lauren Riley."

"If you say so."

The women didn't look convinced.

"I have a restaurant to run." He held up the greens as if they were proof of his claim. "Good luck working with your new chef. When it falls apart, don't say I didn't warn you."

He walked away before either could toss out another sarcastic remark. The last thing Nick expected was for the two kitchen powerhouses to actually like their potential new employer. They were probably only messing with him, and if he were honest, this was the best thing that could happen. Lauren needed help and she clearly wasn't going to take it from him.

Maybe he'd just done her a favor. Getting Mona and Deborah on her side instead of fighting against her would make the reopening go that much smoother. By the time he reached his truck, Nick was patting himself on the back for turning a potential problem into a solution. She would never know it, but he was saving her ass already.

5

SINCE THE TABLES AND CHAIRS WERE FINALLY BEING delivered to the restaurant, Lauren held the staff interviews at the Destination Anchor offices. Roxie checked them in as they arrived and then sent them to Lauren in the conference room one at a time. So far, three dishwashers, six waiters, five waitresses, and five cooks had passed through. All but four had served on the previous staff and none had given Lauren any reason not to hire them.

The interview with the former pastry chef had been the most encouraging. Deborah Prince knew her stuff, and she'd made clear that she was ready and willing to work for Lauren. The enthusiasm was appreciated and had quelled much of the concerns with which she had started the day.

The current interview was going just as well.

"Your level of experience is impressive." Lauren

scanned farther down the resume. "How did you end up on Anchor Island?"

"I came for vacation," Mona Bradwell replied, "and I never left."

Lauren looked up. "Really?"

"Really. I was working in Atlantic City and I hated it. The Marina had a sign on the door that said they were looking for a cook. Me and my daughter, who's off at college now, could live on the ocean, afford a better place than the crappy studio apartment we were in at the time, and within five minutes of meeting Jackson, I knew I could actually enjoy the people I worked with. Have you talked to him yet?"

"No, but he should be in next."

"He's the best," Mona assured her. "I've worked with every kind of chef you can think of. None are as calm and steady as Jackson. He doesn't expect anyone to do what he isn't willing to do himself, and he was always the first one in and the last one out."

At this rate, Lauren wouldn't need to conduct the next interview. "How do you think he would do as second-in-command instead of leading the crew?"

"Oh, Jackson doesn't care much about that. He made the schedules and expedited the orders, but we were all equals in the kitchen." Mona chuckled. "He might be the only man I know who doesn't have an ego the size of Texas. The only chef for sure."

The man sounded too good to be true.

"Speaking of egos," Mona continued, "I caught some

of that little head-to-head you had with Nick Stamatis at the farmer's market."

That had not been Lauren's finest hour. "I shouldn't have let him get to me."

"On the contrary. Deborah and I talked to him after you stormed off and got the gist of things. Good for you for telling him where to shove it."

"What did Nick tell you?"

"That nonsense about all food being equal." The woman shifted to lean her elbow on the back of her chair. "Not in a million years."

Lauren couldn't help but smile. If Jackson proved to be half the paragon his friends made him out to be, then as of that moment, Lauren could relax knowing she had a full, capable staff to help make her dream a reality.

"Ms. Bradwell, how would you feel about the station chef position?"

This was essentially the third-in-command and in larger restaurants would be held by multiple chefs. Considering the size of Pilar's, plus Mona's extensive experience, she was the perfect person to fill such a vital role.

"Chef Riley," she replied with a grin, "you can count on me."

Feeling better than she had in weeks, Lauren rose from her chair and extended a hand. "I look forward to working with you."

Mona rose and accepted the handshake. "Same here. When do you want me to start?"

Since her visit to the farmer's market, Lauren had nearly finished her menu, but she needed the weekend to add the final touches, and then a couple of days to get in the ingredients so they could begin building the dishes.

"Wednesday morning will be good. I'll have Roxie email the details by the end of the day."

They walked together to the door and Lauren showed her out. Waiting outside was Jackson Moore, right on time.

"Jackson, come on in," she said, holding the door for him.

"Thank you, Chef," he said as he stepped through. The way he straightened his tie revealed his nerves, but a genuine smile still reached his eyes.

"Have a seat."

He waited until she'd taken her own seat before following the order. Lauren appreciated his manners.

"You have a lot of fans on this island." Others before Mona had sung his praises. "I hope you can live up to the hype."

A blush rose on his ebony cheeks. "I'm not sure what you've heard, but I'm a hard worker and would like the opportunity to earn my place in your kitchen."

"That's good because this interview is just a formality. Your years with the Marina say a lot about your dedication, but the people who worked with you have convinced me. There's only one issue to discuss.

You were the head chef before, but at Pilar's you would be the deputy chef. Will this be a problem?"

Jackson shook his head. "No, Chef. I'm a big believer that a kitchen doesn't run without a solid team. We all have to pull our weight and I'll do that in whatever capacity you need."

A hundred-pound weight lifted off her shoulders.

"Excellent. Then it's settled." Rising, she added, "The others will start on Wednesday, but I'd like to add one or two staples from the Marina menu to give the locals something familiar. Are you available to come in on Sunday? I'd appreciate your help in determining which dishes to add, but I'll have to try them first."

Her new sous chef stood with a grin. "That's a great idea."

She hated to give Stamatis the satisfaction of following another of his suggestions, but he'd been right. Damn him.

"Then Sunday it is. Leave a list of ingredients with Roxie and I'll pick them up tomorrow. Then we'll meet at the restaurant at nine Sunday morning."

"Yes, Chef."

Jackson left the conference room with a skip in his step and Lauren relaxed back into her chair. She'd done it. She had her first kitchen staff and they were ready to work. Test one over.

Only a thousand more to go.

———

WHEN NICK MOVED to Anchor Island, cell service was spotty at best. In the two years since, nothing had changed. Thankfully, most businesses on the island offered free Wi-Fi so while making calls remained difficult, islanders were still able to stay connected through the needy little devices in their pockets.

Nick wasn't a slave to his phone, but it did come in handy on days like today, when he was stuck in Alex Fielding's waiting room while his grandmother had her regular appointment. Though Nota insisted otherwise, she was no longer a safe driver. That made Nick and Mia her chauffeurs and today was his turn.

The text from Jackson was a welcome distraction. Lauren was bringing back the entire Marina crew plus a few additional team members. She'd also asked for Jackson's input on picking staples from the previous menu to offer on Pilar's. Basically, the woman had taken *all* of Nick's suggestions *after* telling him he could shove them up his ass.

Both annoyed and vindicated, Nick didn't notice the doctor enter the waiting room until he'd tapped him on the shoulder.

"Hey," he said, looking up from his phone. "Is Nota okay?"

"She's fine," Alex said. "Can we talk?"

He glanced around the doctor and didn't see his grandmother. "What's wrong?"

"Nothing," he assured him. "Nota is as healthy as she was when she walked in. This is something else."

Nick relaxed. He and Alex were more acquaintances than friends, but if the doc needed to talk, Nick saw no reason not to oblige him. He followed the man down a narrow hall to a small office on the left. Alex motioned for him to enter first, then followed him in and closed the door.

Either he'd been lying about Nota's health, or the doc had some confession to make. Why he'd choose Nick of all people to tell was a mystery yet to be revealed.

"How are you?" the doctor asked once they'd both taken a seat.

"I'm good. How are you?" he replied, going along with whatever this was.

"I'm okay, thanks for asking. No one ever does that."

"Does what?"

"Asks me how I am."

Right. Was the doc raiding his own medicine cabinet?

"When was the last time you had a physical?" Alex asked next, taking Nick by surprise.

He had to think about his answer. "Before I moved here so I guess a couple of years ago." Leaning forward, he said, "Does Nota need a kidney or something? What is this about?"

"You just had a birthday, didn't you?" the doc said, ignoring the question.

"Yeah, I did."

"Thirty-five?"

"Thirty-six," Nick corrected. "Can we get to the

point? I have to get back to the restaurant."

Alex sighed. "Nota says you think you're going to die soon."

He should have known. "There's nothing you can do about my family history, Fielding. If you're doing this just to make Nota feel better, then fine. We talked." Nick rose from his chair but Alex wasn't finished.

"How old was your father when he died?"

Jaw locked, he replied, "Thirty-seven."

"Was he a relatively healthy man?"

"He ran a restaurant so there wasn't much time for working out, but he was fit."

"Smoker?"

Nick returned to his seat. "He quit ten years before he died."

"I see." Alex tapped a finger on his desk. "How about you? Do you smoke?"

"I never took up the habit."

The doctor opened a manila folder. "Per Nota's request, I looked up your father's and your grandfather's death records. What were you told about their deaths?"

Pissed now, Nick said, "You're sticking your nose where it doesn't belong."

"She's worried about you, Nick. Stress affects her health and her health is my business." Lifting a paper from inside the folder, he said, "Your father died of a heart attack caused by damage brought on by what was most likely a series of silent heart attacks. He may have thought he had indigestion or a pulled muscle." He flipped to another page and continued. "Your grandfather died of a brain aneurysm brought on by high blood pressure."

Nothing Nick didn't already know. "And they both died before they were forty. What's your point?"

Alex leaned his elbows on his desk. "My point is that their deaths were wholly unrelated and unless you're ignoring some severe heartburn or headaches, there's little chance that you will share their fate."

"You don't know that."

"No, I don't." He let out a long sigh. "Contrary to what some physicians like to believe, we are not higher beings. You could walk out of this office and get struck by lightning. Or keel over in your bathroom from a major heart attack there was no way to predict. But that's the case for all of us, Nick. Your chances of dying in the next few years are no higher than mine."

"Again, this is none of your business."

"Is Nota right?" he asked. "Are you so busy waiting to die that you're refusing to live?"

Nick rose again. "Your job is to treat my grandmother. Stick to that and keep your nose out of my life. If you can't do that, I'm sure we can find another doctor who will."

Furious, he left the office to find Nota waiting at the front. She opened her mouth to speak but he cut her off.

"Don't. Just don't."

Her lips snapped shut as she nodded. She knew she'd crossed the line.

He escorted her to the car as gently as ever, and together they rode in silence. Once he'd gotten her home and inside, Nick had only one thing to say.

"Your meddling in my life stops today. Do you understand?"

"I just want you to be happy." When Nick stayed silent, she said, "Yes, I understand."

At the door, he turned. "I love you, Nota. But today you went too far."

"I'm sorry, Nick."

Eyes on the floor, he said, "Me, too," before closing the door behind him.

———

Lauren preferred to do her workouts first thing in the morning, but she'd opted not to hit the gym before the interviews, deciding instead to spend extra time on her appearance. She wasn't a makeup person and kept her hair just long enough to pull up in a ponytail. Today, however, she'd attempted a blowout and applied mascara. There was a truth to dressing the part and for the day she would hire her first-ever kitchen staff, she'd needed the boost of confidence.

To her relief, the interviews had gone better than she'd hoped and come Wednesday the crew—*her* crew— would be in the kitchen. The rest of the day had been spent working on the menu while waiting for the stove delivery, which miraculously arrived as scheduled.

Everything was falling into place easily enough that she couldn't help but feel a sense of imminent doom.

That was the problem with being a pessimist—even when things were good, Lauren still expected the worst.

By eight in the evening, she'd finished the menu except for whatever dishes would be added from the Marina options. Too excited to call it a day, she visited the gym to work off the adrenaline. When she'd arrived, a man and a woman she'd never seen before were the only others using the facility. Most likely nighttime regulars.

Ten minutes into a light jog on the treadmill, with Beyoncé belting a female empowerment anthem through her earbuds, Lauren had worked up both a plan for the week ahead and a good sweat.

She upped the pace to a steady run and as she glanced up from the control board, she noticed Nick Stamatis stepping onto the next treadmill over. There were *eight* machines in the row and all but hers were empty. Could he *not* have picked one of the others?

He offered no greeting and skipped the warm-up levels to go straight to a near sprint. Lauren couldn't help but notice the set of his jaw and the white-knuckled fists pumping forward and back. The man was pissed off about something.

If this was about their last encounter, then he'd just have to pout because she wasn't interested in arguing again, and she sure as hell wasn't going to apologize.

Another minute passed with Nick pumping away

like a man trying to outrun a bear and Lauren pretending he didn't exist. Though she was competitive enough to increase her speed just to prove she could handle the higher pace. Not in the manic way he was, but her pride refused to let him think she couldn't keep up.

Beyoncé rolled into Ed Sheeran and Lauren kept her pace, eyes on the mirror ahead. She told herself not to watch the man beside her, but Nick was difficult to ignore. The white tank, now covered in sweat, revealed well-defined arms and a healthy tuft of dark chest hair. He had great form so he'd probably run track at some point in his life. For a moment she found herself wondering what he'd look like without the shirt on.

Of course, that was the moment their eyes caught in the mirror and Lauren nearly lost her balance. To save her dignity and put space between them, she decided to move on to another machine, but as she cut the treadmill back to a walk, Nick did the same on his. She pretended not to notice.

Normally, she'd do a full five-minute cooldown, but something told her getting away from the Greek god next door was the only way to lower her temperature. She may not have liked him, but she wasn't dead. Roxie had been right. The meddling cook was gorgeous as hell and even hotter when soaked with sweat.

Lauren took the machine down to zero and stepped off to grab a spray bottle and a paper towel. When she returned, Nick was standing still, seemingly waiting for her. He said something she couldn't hear thanks to the music playing in her ears, so she cleaned her machine, ignoring him.

To her surprise, he tugged an earbud away and said, "I know you see me."

"What the—" Lauren fought the temptation to spray him with the cleaner. "What is wrong with you?"

"Let's get a drink," he said.

He could not be serious. "Why would I ever get a drink with you?"

"I hear you hired a staff today. That's your first one, right?"

Of course he knew that already.

"What about it?" she replied.

"That's something to celebrate." Nick pulled a towel off the arm of his machine and wiped his face before wrapping the terry cloth around his neck. "I'll hit the shower and meet you outside in ten minutes."

Before she could refuse, he strolled off toward the men's locker room, leaving her gaping at his back. His wide, muscled back. As if coming out of a trance, Lauren shook her head and said aloud, "There's no way I'm going to do this."

She caught her reflection in the mirror and had another thought.

I can't go looking like this.

Returning the spray bottle and tossing the paper towel, she grabbed her water and phone, then hurried into the locker room to change.

6

LAUREN WAS WAITING OUTSIDE THE GYM ENTRANCE WHEN Nick walked out. He had no idea why he was doing this. He just wanted someone to share a drink with who didn't care enough about him to blow sunshine up his ass. It was safe to assume Lauren Riley fit that description. She'd changed into black jeans and a Red Sox T-shirt under a gray sweat jacket. Her hair was down and wet, so he assumed she'd also taken a quick shower.

"Follow me," he said, breezing past her to reach his truck.

"To where?" she asked, holding her ground.

Nick opened his door. "I know a spot." As he climbed in, Lauren lingered by the entrance, clearly debating whether to join him. Rolling down the passenger window, he said, "It's not a date and I'm not going to attack you. It's drinks on the beach. You in or not?"

Because she couldn't make anything easy, she asked, "What are we drinking?"

"I'm stopping at Louis' Liquor for beer. If that isn't your thing, you can get whatever you want."

"Beer is fine." She strolled to the black GMC parked two spaces down, climbed in, started the vehicle, then glanced his way with a "What are you waiting for?" expression.

He couldn't help but appreciate her no-nonsense attitude. No frills. No artifice. Just you get what you see. Nick liked that.

Louis' wasn't far from the gym and despite it being nine o'clock on a Friday night, traffic was light. Then again, traffic was always light on Anchor except for Sundays when tourists were either arriving or leaving. Lauren parked her Terrain beside his truck, and he walked around to her door. She stared at him for a few seconds before finally rolling the window down.

"What?"

"Are you coming in?"

"You plan to get some fancy-ass beer?"

"Do I look like the fancy-ass beer type?"

She looked him up and down. "I guess not."

He took the assessment as a compliment. "I'll be right back."

With a nod, she rolled the window back up. Minutes later, he returned to his truck with beer in hand and they hit the road again. Nick led her to his cottage and parked in his regular spot. Leaving the vehicle, he noticed Lauren's still sitting on the road. Jogging to her door, he said, "Pull in next to me."

Ignoring the directive, she said, "What is this place?"

"My house," he replied.

"You live here?"

The home was a simple cottage like many on the island. Nothing too fancy for a cook, yet not derelict or run down enough for the look of concern on her face.

"Yeah, I do. We aren't going in though, if that's what you're worried about."

"I'm not afraid of you," she snapped. "My cottage is on this street. I didn't realize we lived near each other."

He hadn't either. "Small island, remember? You pulling in?"

"If we're drinking, I might as well park at my place and walk. Give me two minutes."

Nick stepped away to let her pass but stayed on the road so he could see walk back. Crime on Anchor was virtually nonexistent, but that didn't mean he'd let her walk in the dark without some sort of protection. The main roads in the village had streetlights, but not these side roads closer to the water. He couldn't tell how far down she went, but he was willing to wait as long as necessary for her to return.

When she reached the edge of his property, she noticed him. "Have you been there the whole time?"

"Yeah."

"I'm not a child, Stamatis. I can probably defend myself better than you can."

"You some kind of self-defense expert?"

She drew closer, hands in her pockets and eyes on his cottage. "Something like that. So if we aren't going inside, where are we going?"

"Around back." He headed for his truck to get the beer. "Come on."

Nick led her around the left side of the house, triggering the motion-activated floodlight. He followed the path he'd walked hundreds of times, turning at a rough patch to say, "Watch your footing through here."

"I'm fine," she said, then slipped and snatched a handful of his jacket.

He fought the urge to say I told you so. Twenty feet later they reached their destination and stepped onto the moonlit sand. Nothing but water stretched as far as the eye could see and Nick led her to the Adirondack chairs he kept on the sand not far from his back door.

"Have a seat." He pulled two longnecks from the six-pack. The goal was to have a drink, not to get drunk, as much as he'd rather do the latter. Once she sat, he handed her a bottle and said, "Do you ever wish people would mind their own business?"

Lauren did a spit-take, spewing beer onto the sand. Once she'd wiped her chin, she said, "Did you really just ask me that?"

Nick laughed for the first time in hours. "I guess I have been sticking my nose into your business, but I have good intentions."

"And those are?" she asked.

"What happens with Pilar's affects my friends," he pointed out. "I can't sit back and let it fail when I can do something to help."

Alex's comment about Nick's life affecting Nota's replayed in his mind. He and the doc had similar motives, it seemed.

Shoving her beer bottle into the sand, Lauren rose to her feet. "If you brought me here to talk about how I'm going to fuck up this restaurant, I'm not interested."

"Who said you were going to fuck anything up?"

"You just said you can't let it fail. Like without you the place is doomed." Lauren stormed back toward the path. "Heaven forbid a woman know what she's doing."

"Hold on," he said, catching up to her. "Let's be clear about something. You're a chef. Period. Man. Woman. That's all bullshit. Ingredients don't care what you are. It's what you do with them. About the failing shit, you and I both know how many new restaurants close within the first year, if they make it that long. You're doing this for the first time in a unique place where you have no idea how anything works. All I'm trying to do is give you the knowledge you need to be successful. I'd be doing the same if you were a guy. And if you'd get that damn chip off your shoulder, I wouldn't have to fight you every step of the way."

They stared in silence broken by the waves crashing on the beach.

Lauren broke the stalemate. "Why?"

"Why what?" he said. "I just told you this affects my friends."

"You said yourself, the Marina ran for over thirty years. If I don't make this work, they can fire me and bring in another chef. So why are you so determined to help *me*?"

Time to fess up.

"Because you remind me of someone."

"Please don't tell me I look like some long-lost love of your life."

Nick couldn't help but laugh. "No," he assured her. "I meant myself. If I'm going to tell this story, then I need more beer. Come back and sit if you want to hear it."

Seconds after taking his seat, he heard sand shifting behind him before she joined him once again.

"This better be good."

———

THE ONLY REASON Lauren was still on this beach was Nick's comment that chefs were chefs regardless of gender. In thirteen years of trying to earn her place in the kitchen, she'd never heard anyone say those words. Especially not a man.

"Before I could walk my dad opened his own restaurant," Nick started, his gaze locked on the distant waves. "It was his dream, and he loved every second he spent in that kitchen. Once he started taking me along, I fell in love as well. The smells. The sounds. The speed and choreography of the whole thing. He was my hero and I wanted to be just like him."

Lauren could guess what came next but asked anyway. "What happened to him?"

"He died when I was fifteen."

She'd never known her father, but after losing Mom six months ago, she understood the loss. "I'm sorry."

"Thanks. My mom was left with two teenagers and a restaurant she had no idea how to run, but she found some good people who kept it going until I insisted on taking over." After a long swig of his drink, he sat back in his chair. "I ran it into the ground within nine months."

Guessing this is where he saw their similarities, she asked, "How old were you?"

"Twenty-one."

"I'm not twenty-one," she pointed out.

"No, but you are stubborn as hell."

She couldn't argue with that. "So I'm going to run Pilar's into the ground because I'm stubborn?"

Nick shrugged. "You might make it work. After a few mistakes. Some turnover in the kitchen. But the odds are against you. That's just a reality of the business."

He had no idea what she was capable of, and his assumptions, while accurate in many ways, were also insulting. Lauren may have been a pessimist, but she had confidence in herself and her abilities. She had to because no one else ever had.

"I really am sorry about your dad," she said with

sincerity. "And I'm sorry that you weren't able to keep the restaurant going. But I'm not a kid, and I wouldn't have taken this job if I didn't believe that I could do it. So as I've said before, you run your kitchen, and I'll run mine."

"It's funny," he said, turning her way, the half grin clear in the moonlight. "You opened the interviews to the former staff and you're adding dishes from the Marina menu to the new one. Both suggestions that I made."

"I—" she started, but he cut her off.

"You also didn't mind my help at the farmer's market. Seems like you're willing to take what I offer while at the same time telling me to stay out of your kitchen. You need to make up your mind."

The man went from feminist to jackass in less than a beer. "I never asked you for any of those *suggestions*, though that isn't the word I would use for storming into my restaurant and making demands. As for the menu, yes, I took that one because it's a good idea when the staff who created them would be handling the dishes. Otherwise, I never would have considered it. If you want a 'suggested by Nick Stamatis' added next to each Marina dish in the menu, I'm sure I can have that arranged."

Tipping up her own beer, she finished the bottle, and then stood, leaving the empty on the sand.

"As for the farmer's market, I would have found those connections with or without you. As you mentioned, small island. Now don't bother getting up. I can see myself out."

She'd reached the edge of the house when he said, "Chef."

Lauren stopped, bracing for whatever insult would come next.

"I'm rooting for you," he said.

No sarcasm.

No parting dig.

No warning of imminent doom without him.

Head up, she said, "Thanks," and continued walking.

———

"I THOUGHT I'd find you back here."

Nick closed his eyes. Though Lauren had been gone at least an hour, he remained on the beach replaying their conversation. His professional opinion of her remained the same. She was in over her head. His opinion about her as a person, however, had shifted. She was tough and she believed in herself. That was half the battle right there.

"Let me guess," he said to his sister. "Nota sent you."

"Alex, actually." Mia sat down in the chair Lauren had vacated. "He didn't give me the details, but I get the impression you two had a disagreement."

"If you mean he crossed a line into private family business, then yeah."

She spun in the chair, tossing her legs over the arm

to face him. "What family business are you talking about?"

"Dad and Grandpa's death records."

"Oh." After a brief hesitation, she asked, "What do they say?"

Nick turned to see if she was serious. "You don't know?"

"Grandpa died before we were born. Before Mom and Dad even met, for that matter. And I was ten when Dad passed. No one told me anything."

He couldn't believe she'd never asked. "Mom didn't tell you?"

Mia shook her head. "She just said that Dad was gone and I'd need to help out more because we were on our own."

That sounded like Mom. Her idea of facing life head-on had been to walk into a closet and wait for the storm to pass. She'd grown up in a violent household, and that was how she'd learned to cope, though not until the last few years had he come to understand that.

"Dad died of a heart attack," he told her. "According to Alex, there had been no genetic cause for it, though the doctors never could say why it happened. The guess is that he'd been having smaller ones for a while and didn't know it, but each left a little more damage behind."

Mia rubbed her chest. "How do you have a heart attack and not know it?"

"Alex says they can be mistaken for heartburn."

"That's some serious heartburn. So Grandpa was the same?"

Nick hated talking about this stuff, but after all these years, she had a right to know. "No. He died of a brain aneurysm from high blood pressure."

Her feet hit the sand. "I thought they both died of the same thing. You've been freaking us out all this time and there isn't even a consistent family history?"

"Death is the history, Mia."

Staring as if he'd grown a third eye, she mumbled, "Unbelievable. I've seen pictures of Grandpa. He was overweight, and according to Grandma, ate red meat every day of his life. Of course he had high blood pressure."

"What does that have to do with anything?"

"Look at you." She waved a hand up and down in his direction. "You're the most in shape person I know. You eat healthy, you work out, you've never smoked a day in your life, and you could probably run a marathon tomorrow. If *you're* on the brink of death, then the rest of us are living on borrowed time."

"Dad was healthy."

"Bullcrap. He ate at the restaurant every day, and not the salad. He also smoked."

Collecting his empties, Nick corrected that statement. "He quit ten years before he died."

Mia picked up the bottle Lauren left behind. "That doesn't matter. The damage was done." Before Nick could argue further, she said, "Wait a minute. Someone else was here."

"Lauren Riley." He shoved the empty bottles into the pack with the full ones.

"You were drinking *here* with Lauren Riley?"

Nick stood up. "Yeah. So?"

"But you don't date chefs. That's your rule."

"I'm not dating her. We had a beer and talked about her restaurant."

"In the spot where you bring women to charm them into your bed?"

So maybe he'd created this cozy little area for that purpose, but that didn't mean he couldn't sit out here with a friend. Or an enemy, as Lauren probably considered them. Would he try to get her into bed if she wasn't a chef? Hell yes. She was beautiful, challenging, and sexy as hell when those blues eyes snapped with anger.

He could only imagine how they'd looked filled with desire. But she *was* a chef, so none of this made a difference.

"Don't read into it," he said. "There's nothing going on."

"If you say so, but if you were ever to make an exception to that stupid rule of yours, this would be the time."

Mia popped the last empty into the pack as Nick said, "No exceptions. Besides, for all I know she could be more interested in you."

"She isn't," his sister said without hesitation.

"How do you know?"

She sighed. "I just know."

On their way into the house, he asked, "What about Henri?"

He felt her tense up beside him. "What about her?"

"Why haven't you asked her out?"

That earned him a smack on the arm. "You know why."

"She's let you know she's interested. Go for it already."

"I can't ask her to sneak around like that."

Nick stopped at the edge of the porch. "Mia, just tell Nota already. She loves you. She deserves to know who you really are."

Ignoring him, she marched up the stairs. "You worry about your love life and I'll worry about mine."

Joining her at the top, he bumped her with his shoulder. "Neither of us has a love life, remember?"

As he'd hoped, she laughed. "At least I have a good reason."

Not wanting to start this again, Nick motioned toward the door. "Get inside. I've got leftover shrimp alfredo in the fridge."

"Oh, I am on that."

By the time Nick tossed the empty bottles into the recycle bin, Mia had the alfredo warming in the microwave. No one on the island would probably believe that his sister and grandmother were the only women who'd stepped foot inside his house in months. So long as he maintained the playboy reputation, no one asked any annoying questions about finding a wife or starting a family.

Two things Nick was in no position to do.

7

LAUREN'S DAY WITH JACKSON HAD GONE BETTER THAN she'd hoped. They'd chosen three dishes from the Marina menu, keeping them as close to the originals as possible while adding small touches that elevated them to the level of the rest of the Pilar's menu. Two included seafood while the third, a roasted beet and butternut squash concoction, would appeal to their vegetarian customers.

The best part of her day had been the revelation that was Jackson Moore.

Despite the changes she'd made to the kitchen, the man moved through the space with a casual ease. There was nothing rushed or intense about him—unlike other chefs she'd worked with—but he also didn't move too slowly either. He was a font of knowledge about flavors, especially anything involving seafood, and was an expert on the subject of the islanders.

They discussed what the locals preferred versus the tourists, while exploring what might be lacking on the island that they could provide. If all went well, Pilar's would fill those gaps and become the place to eat for both natives and visitors alike. Jackson also suggested they add a few kid's menu items, since Anchor was a family destination and many parties would include the little ones. That was something Lauren hadn't considered, but the more she learned about Anchor, the more her vision shifted to accommodate her new surroundings.

The next two days had been spent finding ingredients for when the full cooking staff arrived on Wednesday morning. A day that did not prove as positive or productive as those before it.

"Are you sure you're okay?" asked Roxie. They were standing at the hostess station reviewing the menu design now that the offerings had been finalized.

"I'm fine," Lauren said through clenched teeth.

On a normal day, the sounds of an active kitchen—the tap, tap, tap of a knife on a cutting board and the sizzle of oil in a hot pan—were like a symphony to her. But today, after four hours of having to correct and discuss and debate every damn thing, she wanted nothing but silence.

"Fine enough that you're going to grind your teeth to dust." Roxie took her hand and led Lauren to a nearby table. "Sit and tell me what's going on."

Desperate for a confidant, she lowered her voice and

whispered, "If I hear the words 'But that's not how we've always done it' one more time, I'm going to start stabbing people."

"Ah." Roxie nodded in understanding. "That is one downfall to hiring the old staff. They've been together for a long time and are set in their ways, I'm sure."

Lauren had believed their teamwork and experience would be a benefit, not an obstacle.

"I have to give Jackson credit," she said. "He's reminded them three times that this is my kitchen now, but I only have ten days to make this work, Roxie, and I can't fight them every step of the way."

"I guess you could replace them," she whispered. "But that would be kind of mean now that they've started."

She could just imagine Nick flying through the door in a rage if she tried that. Not that it was an option. They'd received few applications outside the established staff, and most of those had little to no experience. She couldn't launch her menu with a kitchen full of rookies.

"I don't want to replace them. I just need to get them to trust me."

Lauren knew her way around the kitchen, and she knew her food, but people skills had never been in her repertoire. Damn it, this wasn't supposed to be so hard.

Roxie leaned back and crossed her arms. "Most of my jobs before moving to Anchor were temp work or retail, and no one in retail cares enough to argue how to do anything. Do you have any chef friends back home that could give you tips?"

No one from Lauren's past was likely to take her call. Ironically, she had a reputation for not being a team player. Nothing like karma coming around to bite her in the ass. Running her own kitchen was supposed to be her dream come true. Her team. Her food. No one to tell her she didn't belong. Yet on the first day in her own kitchen—she was once again the odd one out.

Unwilling to share the details of her past, Lauren shook her head. "I'll figure it out." Tapping the sample menu on the right, she said, "Let's go with this, but I like the font on the cream one better. It's easier to read."

They were ordering simple card stock menus so they had the flexibility to add and delete dishes as the seasons changed.

"You've got it." They both rose from the table as Roxie said, "What about Nick Stamatis? He was the new guy at Dempsey's not that long ago. He must have ideas for how to run an established team."

Lauren nearly groaned at the idea. After repeatedly telling him to stay out of her business, there was no way she would go crawling to him now.

With a noncommittal shrug, she said, "I'll think about it."

Roxie left and Lauren returned to the kitchen, catching the conversation inside before pushing through the swinging door.

"Why can't we do things the way we've always done them?" a voice asked.

"Because this is Chef Riley's kitchen and she says to do it her way," Jackson answered.

"Her way just makes it way more complicated. She needs to let us do what we know."

"There's nothing wrong with learning a new way. If she wants us to do things differently, then she must have a good reason for it."

Lauren made a mental note to give Jackson an immediate raise.

"And why are you all up her ass?" asked a different voice. This one sounded like Mona. "You ran this kitchen for fifteen years, and we were a team already. We don't need her coming in here and changing shit. We know what we're doing."

"I need this job, Mona. Nobody else on the island is hiring full time and if I don't make this work, Denise and I will have to leave Anchor for good. I don't like her any more than you do, but I don't have a choice."

Like a bullet through the door, his words knocked the wind out of her. Anger, hurt, and utter defeat sent bile into her throat as she braced an arm against the wall to hold herself up. None of them wanted her here. None of them wanted to work for her. They just wanted a paycheck and were willing to stomach the new bitch of a chef to get one.

After several deep breaths, Lauren lifted her chin and pushed through the door. "That's all for today. Everyone can go home."

All eyes turned her way as Mona said, "We have another four hours to go."

"No, you don't," Lauren corrected. "We've done enough for today."

"But we just—"

"I said go home," she snapped. After clearing her throat, she added in a more level tone, "We'll start again tomorrow."

The crew exchanged glances ranging from confused to concerned, but they slowly followed the order. Aprons were removed, knives were sheathed, and not another word was said.

Once Lauren was alone in the kitchen, she braced her hands on the stainless-steel prep counter and concentrated on keeping her emotions in check. She hadn't cried since Mom died, and she wasn't going to shed a tear today. Once her breathing steadied, she straightened, knowing what she had to do.

If Nick told her to fuck off, it would be her own damn fault.

———

He'd been home long enough to shower and dive back into his current car show on Netflix when the knock sounded at his door. Assuming it was Mia, Nick swept it open, saying, "What?"

But the person on his doorstep was not his sister.

Lauren held a six-pack out in front of her. "Peace offering. Can I come in?" Temporarily stunned, he stared at the beer in silence until she said, "Sorry, I shouldn't have come." She spun on her heel and Nick snapped out of his daze.

"No, it's fine. Come on in."

She lingered on the porch. "Are you sure?"

"I'm sure." He stepped back to let her enter and the scent of vanilla filled his senses as she passed. "Have a seat."

There was no fancy foyer in his house, so the entrance opened into the living room. Nick padded around her and snagged the remote off the coffee table to press pause on the show, then he turned to find her standing at the end of the couch.

"Anywhere is fine." Pointing to the beer, he said, "Are those to share?"

"Oh, yeah." Lauren set the pack on the coffee table and perched on the edge of a chair.

His furniture—the sofa and two bulky leather chairs—created a U-shape around the coffee table and he settled back where he'd been before on the couch.

"What's up?"

"First, I owe you an apology."

He nearly made a joke about where the real Lauren might be, but the tension in her eyes stopped him. "Okay."

"You've been trying to help me, and I've been too proud to let you."

Since she'd taken nearly all of his advice, that wasn't quite true, but this didn't seem the time to point that out. As a group, chefs were trained not to show weakness, and few liked to admit when they were wrong. Points to her for doing so.

"Like you said, you didn't ask for my input," he replied. "I should have given you more credit."

Lauren snorted. "If today is any indication, I should have shut up and listened." She whisked a bottle from the cardboard pack, twisted off the top with one smooth motion, and tossed it onto the coffee table. "They hate me."

"Who hates you?" he asked, following her lead and snagging a bottle for himself.

"All of them. Even Jackson. He's just being cooperative so he can keep living on the island."

Curious, Nick asked, "How do you know that?"

She took a long swig before answering. "Because I heard them in the kitchen. They didn't know I was on the other side of the door to overhear their enlightening and honest conversation. Though I suppose I knew even before that. They pushed back on everything I said today." Tapping the bottle in time with the words, she added, "Every. Fucking. Thing."

He couldn't say he was surprised, but he'd expected the first rifts to start a week or so in, not on the first day.

"What were you wanting them to do?"

"Normal prep," she said, dropping back in the chair. "But this station was over there before. Why did I have to move it over here? And the line ran that way not this way. And why did the bins have to be over there when before they were over here?" The bottle jerked through the air as she ranted. "I don't give a damn where this shit was before. Why can't they just put it where I tell them?"

Seeing the problem, he asked, "Would the way they had it before work for the flow you need?"

"What?" she said, squinting his way. "Are you saying they're right?"

This was delicate ground and if he didn't want to wear that beer, Nick would need to tread lightly.

"I'm just trying to get the whole picture. Are you having them change what they're used to because it's a better setup, or because the old way isn't your way?"

She snarled, then huffed as steely-blue eyes dropped to her bottle. "I suppose the way they had it before *could* work, but it isn't how I envisioned my kitchen."

"So long as they create your food to your standards, what does it matter where the mise en place is done?"

"The logistics of the kitchen is not the problem," she mumbled. "They don't trust me."

"Do you trust them?" he asked, pretty sure he knew the answer.

"I don't trust anyone," she admitted.

"Then there's your problem."

"Look," she said, sitting up and setting her beer on the table. "Other than what Jackson made me over the weekend, I've never tasted the food they're used to making. And I didn't get to taste anything today either because I sent them home early after hearing them agree about what a bitch I am. How do I know if they can cook my food?"

Nick scratched his head, unsure how to explain this in a way she might hear it.

"How many restaurants have you worked in?" he asked.

"A lot, why?"

"So each time you got hired, they had to believe that you could do the job, having nothing to go on but your resume."

"I'm a trained chef. Of course I could do the job."

"Then you expected them to trust you."

"Yes."

"But you won't trust the people who served hundreds if not thousands of meals out of that same kitchen you're trying so hard to reshape."

He could almost see the light go on over her head. "That was a totally different menu," she argued, not ready to admit defeat.

"That was sauces and proteins and vegetables cooked over a heat source. We are all doing the same thing, Lauren. Some better than others, yes, but we're still just preparing food to make people happy."

"Fine. Then tell me, oh kitchen guru, how do I get them to trust me?"

"Trust goes both ways. Just as you're making them earn yours, you have to earn theirs."

She scoffed. "So what? We stand in a circle and do

trust exercises?"

Not a bad idea, actually. "Yes, that's exactly what you do." Nick left the couch to search for a business card on his side table. "Here it is."

"Here's what?"

He handed her the card. "Defying Gravity Adventure Park up in Nags Head. They specialize in this kind of thing. It's basically a giant jungle gym with suspension bridges and zip lines. Teams work together to complete the obstacles, some of which are fifty feet off the ground. If you can't learn to trust each other up there, then there's no hope of it ever happening."

Blinking, her eyes shifted from the business card to his face and back again. "You want me to take my kitchen staff to an obstacle course?"

"Why not?"

"Because crossing some suspension bridge has nothing to do with cooking a scallop to the proper temperature."

Nick plucked the card from her hand. "You came to me this time. If you don't like my ideas, then you're on your own."

"Wait."

She bolted from the chair and reached around him for the card. Nick turned at the same time and she landed against his chest, her cobalt-blue eyes nearly level with his, her scent, sweet and warm, surrounding him. His free hand cupped her waist as she stood pressed against him with her lips parted and a soft hue rising on her cheeks.

"I didn't say no," she murmured as her eyes dropped to his lips.

The invitation was too much. Nick told himself to step away, but when her tongue trailed along her bottom lip, he forgot all the reasons this couldn't happen. Leaning forward, he pressed his mouth to hers, feeling more than hearing her soft sigh. Her arms slid up his chest to wrap around his neck and the moment she opened for him, allowing him to deepen the kiss, Nick's cell phone went off, blasting "Born To Be Wild" through the living room.

Lauren leaped away as if scalded, nearly falling backward over the coffee table. He reached to catch her, but she managed to right herself and retreat to several feet away. They stared in silence, her slender fingers pressed to her lips as his phone continued to blare.

"You should get that," she finally said, and Nick wanted to hurl the damn phone against the wall.

Instead, he crossed to the kitchen counter and answered it. "What?" he said upon seeing his sister's name on the screen.

"What's wrong with you?" she asked. "You told me to call to talk about Mom's birthday present. So I'm calling."

He'd forgotten about that. "Sorry, I was in the middle of something."

"Do you need me to let you go?" Mia asked.

Unsure how to answer, Nick turned to check on Lauren and found the room empty. Moments later, his front door click shut.

Running a hand through his hair, he crossed the living room, saying, "Let me call you back."

Without waiting for a reply, he ended the call on his way outside but there was no one around. No retreating taillights. No sound of footsteps on gravel. She must have walked, but other than knowing she lived farther down the lane, Nick had no idea which cottage was hers. Only three others on the street had permanent residents, leaving the other six as rentals, and he wasn't about to knock on random doors.

Returning inside, he looked at the phone in his hand. The first thing he did was turn down the damn ringer. Then he fired off a text to Mia saying he'd talk to her tomorrow. She'd only ask questions he didn't feel like answering right now. Hell, he didn't even know the answers. What just happened had been mutual but stupid. He had his rules for a reason.

Retrieving his beer and the remote, Nick dropped onto the couch with a sigh and spotted the adventure park card on the floor. Picking it up, he heard her words in his head.

I don't trust anyone.

Everyone trusted someone. And if they didn't, they had a good reason. So what was hers?

He tossed the card onto the table and pressed play on

his show. Lauren Riley was none of his business, and if he had any sense at all, he'd leave her the hell alone. Especially after tonight. But then he caught her scent still lingering in the air and considered taking Mia's suggestion and making an exception.

8

LAUREN PAUSED AT THE ENTRANCE TO PILAR'S AND TOOK a deep breath. She'd messaged Jackson first thing that morning to say she'd be late and that he should let the rest of the staff inside. They were to have a seat in the dining room and wait for her.

None of this was because she'd slept in or hit traffic —a laughable idea on this sleepy little island—but due to an impromptu morning meeting with Will Navarro.

Though she'd left Nick's place without the business card—for obvious reasons—a simple internet search had brought up the adventure park website. Lauren had gathered the information she needed to make the presentation to Will, and then tossed and turned all night imagining her boss laughing her out of the office.

Not that she'd blame her. This *was* a crazy idea, but Nick had been right. Lauren had watched the video on the park website and giant jungle gym didn't do the place justice. She'd never had a fear of heights, but then she'd also never climbed five stories up and attempted to travel from one pole to the next via a dozen chairs suspended in the air by three ropes.

Taking on this challenge would either mold the team as one or make it clear she'd need a whole new staff.

The loss of sleep had been for nothing since Will approved the plan immediately. She'd not only agreed to pay their entry fees, but each staff member would be paid their normal daily wages. Now to convince the team to cooperate.

"Good morning," she said upon stepping inside. "Thank you for waiting."

"Morning," the crew said in unison and with the expected amount of enthusiasm, which wasn't much.

Setting her hurt feelings aside, Lauren was determined to push forward and get everyone on the same page. Preferably *her* page. The previous evening had brought two realizations—compromise was sometimes necessary and Nick Stamatis was an amazing kisser.

If she was honest, Lauren would admit that the latter had contributed the most to her inability to sleep, but no one needed to know that. Especially not Nick. The kiss had taken her by surprise. She couldn't remember the last time she'd been with a man, and Nick Stamatis wasn't just *any* man. He was the epitome of tall, dark, and handsome—so cliché and yet so irresistible.

She'd taken the coward's way out—not her proudest

moment—but retreat had been necessary to keep from jumping his bones. When passing his house on the way to meet Will that morning, she'd stomped on the gas as if he might come out and catch her. Proof that she could not think rationally where Nick was concerned.

Of all the cottages on this island, why did Will have to give her one so close to his?

"I think we all can agree that yesterday did not go well," she said, addressing the room. "I'm at a disadvantage in that you all know each other, but you don't know me. Despite how some of you may feel, I *am* the head chef in this kitchen. If I want something done a certain way, it's for a reason, but at the same time I understand that for many years this was *your* kitchen and you did things differently."

Lauren paused long enough to hear a huff come from the back of the room. Her eyes caught Mona's and the woman had the grace to look away.

"We have ten days before we open the doors. That means we don't have time to dance around each other so we're going to speed things up. Today, I'm willing to discuss the setup of the kitchen. You show me your way and we see if it works for what I want to accomplish."

Several sat up straighter, signaling she had their attention. Now, for the twist.

"Tomorrow morning, I need the cooking staff to be here by six thirty. We're taking a field trip." Confused glances were exchanged as a low murmur developed. Lauren waited for them to grow quiet before continuing. "We're visiting the Defying Gravity Adventure Park in Nags Head to do some team building exercises."

"You cannot be serious," said Deborah.

"I don't think so," echoed Mona.

"This is mandatory," Lauren cut in, gaining their attention once more. "Look, I don't want to have to change crews. At this point, I'm not even sure I could without delaying the opening. But if we're going to be in the fire together, then we need to trust each other. You'll be paid for the time we're gone just as you would be if you were working in the kitchen. This is another workday, except instead of knives, we'll have harnesses and zip lines."

No one spoke for several seconds until Jackson finally said, "I'm in, Chef."

"You're afraid of heights," Mona reminded him.

The man turned to face his coworker. "Chef is right. We have to work together and if she's willing to give us another chance after yesterday, then I'm willing to strap on a harness and make this work. What are you going to do, quit? You know you don't want to lose this opportunity. You've seen the menu. Where else are we going to get the chance to make food like this?"

Lauren hadn't expected such support after the "I don't like her either" comment the day before. Then again, Jackson had made it clear that he needed this job.

"I shouldn't have to haul my ass up a rope ladder to prove I can cook," Mona argued.

"And I shouldn't have to argue over where a garbage can goes," Lauren cut in, "but here we are."

Mona went silent and Deborah said, "Count me in. I've always wanted to zip line. Even better if I can get paid to do it."

The remaining four cooks followed suit until Mona was the only dissenting voice.

"Well?" Jackson said. "Are you with us or are you out?"

"Shit. You know I'm going," she said, her bottom lip jutted out. "I don't like it, but I'll do it."

"Good." Lauren rose from her chair as a voice sounded from the back.

"I want to go."

She looked up to find Brendon the dishwasher wearing a hopeful expression.

"Sorry, but I only got approval for the cooking staff." When he looked defeated, she said, "Maybe if we have a successful launch, I can get Will to send the rest of the staff."

"Yes."

The team headed for the kitchen while Jackson approached Lauren. "I owe you an apology, and I just wanted to say thank you for giving us another shot. After how we acted yesterday, I'm not sure we deserve one."

Not ready to trust him just yet, Lauren nodded. "Apology accepted. Why don't we consider this the first day and move on?"

"Yes, Chef." He hesitated another moment and she waited for him to say what was on his mind. "I really am afraid of heights. How far up are we talking?"

She considered lying lest he back out, but she couldn't be that mean. "The top is fifty feet but some are as low as ten." Jackson swayed as if she'd hit him with a blow dart. "There might be something we can do on the ground," Lauren added, afraid he might faint. If this was his reaction just hearing about the place, then tomorrow was going to be a real challenge.

He rubbed the back of his neck. "That would be good. But I'll do my best to keep up with the group. No matter how high."

"I appreciate that. Thanks for convincing them to go."

"Ah, they'd have gone. We all want to be here. We just aren't used to change, that's all."

And she wasn't used to compromise. They all had something to learn.

"Then let's see what we can keep the same, shall we?"

With a grin, he said, "Yes, Chef," and took off toward the kitchen.

"WHY DIDN'T you call me back?" Mia demanded as she stomped into Nick's kitchen. He'd worked the lunch shift after a long, sleepless night and the last thing he wanted to do was to deal with his sister.

"I was busy." He slid the creamy sea urchin soup her way. "Eat."

Lifting her spoon, she took a deep sniff over the soup. "How did I get so lucky to have a chef for a brother?"

"You must have done something good in a former life."

The first bite went in and she sighed. "Something *really* good. Now back to my question. What happened last night?"

"I had unexpected company."

"Who was it?" Mia asked, filling her spoon for another bite.

"Nobody." Nick finished filling his own bowl, grabbed a spoon, and rounded the island to take a seat at the table across from his sister. "What are we going to get for Mom?"

"You're being suspicious," she said, ignoring his attempt to change the subject. "Who is *nobody*?"

Realizing he forgot the drinks, he returned to the kitchen. "Not everything is your business, little one."

She stared him down as he set a soda in front of her. "You haven't called me that since I was twelve, and you only ever did it when there was something you didn't want me to rat you out on."

"Who are you going to rat me out to?" he asked. "I'm a little beyond the getting grounded age."

Watching him closely, Mia squinted in concentration. "You had a woman here."

"That's none of your business."

"You *definitely* had a woman here. Please tell me you didn't finally give in to Roberta from the grocery store."

Roberta Silverman had been hitting on Nick for more than a year. He'd been careful not to encourage her since learning that she'd been married three times already and was on a mission to land her next significant other. She was also about twenty years older than him by his best estimation. Not that Nick had anything against older women, per se, but two decades was a little out of his comfort zone.

"I have not given in to Roberta and we are here to talk about a birthday present. Can we please stick to the topic?"

"But this is so much juicier," she pressed. "You sounded pissed when you answered, so I must have interrupted something good. Not that I want the gory details." Mia held a hand up palm out. "I just want to know who she is."

Nick drank what was left of his soda and rose from his chair. "Let it go." He opened the pantry to toss in the empty bottle and found the recycle can full. "I need to empty this. You better have a gift idea when I get back."

"You're seriously no fun."

Carrying the plastic bin through the house, he stepped out the front door and followed the porch to the end where he kept his cans. He'd just tipped the contents into the larger can when Mia stepped onto the porch. "Your phone is ringing. Why do you have it on vibrate only?"

As she handed him the cell, a black SUV pulled down the road. He glanced up to see Lauren through the side window. They locked eyes before she hit the gas and sped off. Nick stepped off the porch and watched her go, hoping to see which cottage was hers.

"So you *are* breaking your own rule," Mia murmured.

"What?" Nick spun to see her watching him with a knowing grin and remembered the phone vibrating in his hand. The name on the screen told him Jackson was calling. "Go eat," he snapped, answering the call.

Mia stuck out her tongue before prancing back inside.

"Hello?"

"Nick, buddy, you aren't going to believe this. Chef Riley has us all going to some crazy adventure park tomorrow."

Watching Lauren cut him a quick look before shuffling inside the fourth cottage down, he replied, "I wonder where she got that idea?"

———

IN THE MONTH that Lauren had been on Anchor Island, no one had knocked on her door. Until tonight. It didn't take a genius to guess who she'd find on the other side. She would answer, because he'd watched her come home and knew she was there, but she would not invite him inside.

Still, she fluffed her hair and checked her teeth in the mirror that hung near the door. She'd grabbed a salad on her way home and didn't want to face Nick looking as if she'd been gnawing on a head of lettuce.

Doing her best to look as if butterflies weren't creating a funnel cloud in her stomach, she opened the door with what she hoped was a blank expression. "Hello."

"Hey," he said, his hands tucked deep in the front pocket of his jeans. The ever-present scruff along his jaw was darker than usual, as if he'd decided to let it grow out. She hoped that wasn't the case. "Can I come in?" he said.

Send him home, ordered her rational, sensible side.

"Sure." Lauren stepped back to let him enter and the scents of salt water and woodsy pine mingled like an erotic cocktail that evoked both clean and not so clean images in her mind. "What can I do for you?"

Help you take that shirt off perhaps?

Lauren closed her eyes and told her libido to calm down. *The man kissed you one time. Chill the hell out.*

Nick seemed to be assessing her furnishings, which weren't really hers at all. The place had come furnished, of course. The coral-pink couches, navy coffee table, and Kelly-green bureau were more colorful than she'd ever pick for herself, yet she'd gotten used to the splashes of color, which stood out against the all-white walls.

"You left in a hurry last night," he said.

If in a hurry he meant in a dead run like the coward that she was, then yes she did.

"You had a call so I showed myself out."

Brown eyes caught hers. "Are you really pretending that nothing happened before that call?"

"We kissed," she said matter-of-factly. "Since you said you don't date chefs, I thought I'd save us both from this conversation."

Partially true. She'd really wanted to save herself from looking like a fool when he reminded her of his dating policies. Not that she wanted to date him. Lauren didn't do relationships. But a woman needed to scratch an itch now and then and she'd bet anything that Nick would be an excellent scratcher.

"There are exceptions to every rule," he mumbled, walking farther into the house. "Nice place. I haven't seen the rentals since they were redone after the hurricane."

Still dazed by the exceptions comment, Lauren said, "The hurricane?"

"Hurricane Deloris. Tore through in November and left a good bit of destruction in her wake. I lost some shingles but this cottage and the next two were ripped up pretty good." He glanced into the room off the living room, which was her bedroom. "Looks like they updated during the renovations."

Uncomfortable with the man so close to her bed, she pulled the bedroom door closed. "That explains why everything looks so new."

Nick proceeded into the kitchen as if on a tour and Lauren followed close behind, still pondering the exception thing. Was he suggesting that he'd make an exception *for her*?

"Jackson says you took my advice."

"Your advice?" she said, struggling to keep up. Did she want to be an exception? *Hell, yes*, her libido responded.

"About the adventure park. He's pretty freaked out actually. The man's afraid of heights."

"Yes, I heard."

Running his hand along the edge of the countertop, he said, "Nice prep space but the electric stove is a shame."

Lauren had felt the same when she'd moved in. Chefs preferred to cook over an open flame. Better control that way.

Unable to take this much longer, she said, "Nick, why are you here?"

He leaned his exceptional ass against the edge of the counter and crossed his arms. "I don't do relationships," he said, tossing her off-balance once again.

They had that in common. "Neither do I," she replied.

"Really?"

"You aren't the only one with policies," Lauren

explained. "Relationships require trust and I've already told you that I don't trust anyone. Given the opportunity, people will let you down every time. Life is less messy if you don't give them the chance."

Strong fingers scratched his scruffy chin. "That's a cynical view of the world."

"That's called lessons learned," she corrected. "Now you know my reason. What's yours?"

He took several seconds to consider his answer and finally said, "Mine is similar but reversed. I don't want anyone to get attached when I know I'd let them down."

An enlightened answer, especially for a man. "Very evolved of you."

"So we're on the same page then?" Nick asked, and she assumed he meant they'd just agreed to nip this kissing thing in the bud.

"We are."

"Good." Shifting off the counter, he closed the space between them to stand entirely too close. "How about you come to my place tomorrow night and tell me how the day went?"

"But we—"

"Are two grown adults who know exactly where we stand," he finished for her. "I'll have a late dinner ready. Ten o'clock?"

Realizing he was offering the no-strings-attached scratch that she most desperately wanted, Lauren relaxed.

"I'll bring the beer."

9

A STORM MOVED THROUGH OVERNIGHT, STIRRING THE seas and leaving a chill in the air. Lauren blamed the weather for keeping her awake, but the real culprit was Nick Stamatis and his promising invitation. She couldn't pinpoint exactly when he'd gone from aggravating nuisance to potential bedmate, but she'd definitely turned that corner if her overactive imagination was any indication.

She'd given up her futile attempts to sleep well before dawn, opting for a lukewarm shower and a strong coffee before heading to Pilar's for the meetup. When Lauren arrived, the sun had yet to come up and she found Axel Stedmeyer waiting alone on the entrance stairs. She hadn't expected the quiet young man to be there before her.

The day before had gone well enough considering the entire team had been on edge. Lauren made some compromises regarding the layout and flow of the kitchen, and Axel had offered one of the better suggestions while also backing Lauren several times. He seemed to be a hard worker, spoke only when necessary, and ignored the opportunity to flirt with the dishwasher who batted her eyelashes whenever he was around.

Surfer boys with man buns were clearly the girl's weakness, but Axel either didn't notice or simply wasn't interested. So long as the unrequited love didn't cause problems in her kitchen, Lauren was happy to let the pair work things out on their own.

The rest of the crew trickled in, all well before the given time of six thirty. Another of the Navarro entities —a water sports business called Anchor Adventures— provided the shuttle bus that carried them up the Outer Banks to their destination. The trip should have taken less than three hours, but the ferry had been delayed due to rough waters and they reached the adventure park fifteen minutes late. Lauren had called ahead and the staff assured her that they'd honor the reservation.

When they stepped out of the van, the realization of what they were about to do hit home. Off in the distance stood a tangled monstrosity the likes of which Lauren had never seen before. The pictures on the website had not prepared her for the real thing.

A five-story round tower loomed in the center with a dozen poles standing in a circle around it. There must have been hundreds of ropes running not just between the poles but crisscrossing to and from the tower at different levels. The letters OBX hung between two poles.

Not until she moved to the area had she learned that this was the local abbreviation for Outer Banks.

"What fresh hell is this?" mumbled Mona, holding a hand above her eyes to block the sun.

"An adventure park," Lauren replied, trying to sound confident. As if the sight ahead didn't make her want to pee her pants. "They don't call it Defying Gravity for nothing, I guess."

Lauren always assumed she was fine with heights, but that theory had never been tested. As a kid, there'd been no money for anything that could remotely be called an adventure, and from the age of eighteen she'd been working in restaurant kitchens, often up to eighty hours a week, which left no time for vacations. She'd never been to an amusement park or even gone hiking.

"We're going up there?" Jackson muttered with a mixture of awe and fear in his voice.

"It looks fun," Axel said.

Nothing about this looked fun and a wave of nausea threatened. Closing her eyes, Lauren breathed through her nose. This was no time to show weakness. She was their leader, and today she would have to prove it.

Opening her eyes, she spun to face her team. "Are we ready?" Her voice cracked but she put on a brave face.

"Have any of you been here before?" asked Hermie, their driver. After a collective no, he said, "You can't take phones or anything that can fall out of your pockets.

Take your IDs but leave the rest in the bus and I'll make sure they're safe."

"Where will we put our IDs then?" asked Dodge Caldwell, one of the younger chefs.

"I've got my fanny pack," Penny Lee offered, pointing to the bright-pink pouch on her hip. "Y'all can stick 'em in here."

Of course Penny had a solution. She'd been working under Deborah in pastry for more than a year, having moved up within weeks of being hired to bus tables. When Axel's apron had ripped the day before, Penny had retrieved a needle and thread from her car and sewed him up. When Deborah's hair band had broken, Penny offered the spare one from her wrist.

Deborah called her the kitchen Girl Scout, prepared for anything, and the nickname fit.

"Are those chairs?" Brit Davenport asked as they started walking toward the check-in center.

"Chairs of death," Mona answered. "Are we really doing this?"

"We are," Lauren replied.

Fifteen minutes later, they were harnessed up with helmets in place, standing on the observation deck that was the last stop before entering the eye of the storm. Literally. That's what the park called the center tower. Every pole sported a bright-red flag, all of which were whipping in the wind. In ground school—the quick training they'd gone through to prepare them for their day—they'd learned that the top-level course was closed due to the high winds coming off the water.

Jackson had breathed an audible sigh of relief, and Lauren echoed the sentiment, though silently.

"It's time to break into teams," said Everette, their escort.

Lauren had not been aware of this tidbit. "But we're here to do team building exercises," she reminded him. "As a whole team."

"There are exercises you'll do later on the ground that will include everyone, but for the courses you have to be in teams of three or fewer. As you learned earlier, there can be no more than two people on a platform at once." He pointed up to a small disc-looking thing wrapped around the closest pole. "That's a platform. And there can only be one person on the course at a time." Everette indicated a series of blue half-barrels strung together between two poles. "Anything between the poles is an obstacle."

"We have to walk across those things?" Deborah asked.

To which Mona mumbled, "Oh, hell no."

Before Everette could answer, a child no more than ten years old breezed across the barrels and gave a whoop of joy on the other side.

"If a kid can do it, we can do it," said Axel.

The group murmured their agreement with little conviction or enthusiasm.

"You three on a team," the escort said, indicating

Jackson, Penny, and Axel. "Then you three." He pointed at Dodge, Deborah, and Brit.

This left Lauren and Mona as the final, two-person team.

"I'll go with Deborah," Mona said, physically edging Brit out of the way.

"Sorry," he said, "that's not how it works. You don't get to pick your teammates."

"Why not?" Mona demanded.

"Because you're more likely to pick a person you're already comfortable with and that defeats the purpose of team building."

As much as Lauren would rather not team up with Mona, she couldn't argue with the logic.

They made their way down the narrow pier-like walkway into the center tower, where they were connected to the belay system, the lifeline that ran through the entire structure and kept them from plummeting to their deaths. Only staff could disconnect them so there was no turning back now.

"The team who gets through their course the quickest gets an advantage in the ground challenges," Everette said, "so keep that in mind."

"We're competing?" Brit asked.

"You are." To Jackson's team, he said, "You guys can start out that way."

Axel was in the lead and as he stepped out, Jackson tossed one last *save me* look Lauren's way. She gave him an uncharacteristic thumbs-up, as much for her own benefit as for his.

"Team two can head out that way," Everett said.

Deborah went first, with Dodge and Brit close behind. That left Lauren alone with Mona, who looked more likely to throw her off a ledge than to work with her.

"You two start that way."

Lauren was in front and before she took two steps, Mona asked, "What if we get stuck?"

Everette, who had clearly encountered plenty of scaredy-cats in his day, smiled as one would when trying to calm a spastic three-year-old on a sugar rush. "Keep putting one foot in front of the other and you'll be fine, but if you decide you don't want to continue at any point in the course, there's a zip line from every post that leads right back here."

Mona tugged on the strap that connected her to the belay. "This is going to hold my ass?"

His grin grew wider. "It will hold all of you."

They moved into motion again and as Lauren sct foot on the ledge that led to the barrels—because of course they'd gotten that one first—Mona leaned close and whispered, "If I go down, I'm taking you with me."

Her competitive side coming alive, Lauren said, "If we go down, then the other teams win. Do you want that to happen?"

After a brief hesitation, her partner replied with a succinct, "No."

"Me neither. Let's do this."

———

A WEEK HAD PASSED since Nota's doctor's appointment and Nick hadn't spoken to his grandmother since, but she'd left a message on his phone the night before asking him to come for lunch. The invitation had been more of a demand than a request. He hadn't avoided her on purpose. As April progressed, more tourists arrived on the island. That meant more business at the restaurant, which extended Nick's hours in both the kitchen and the office, making sure they had the supplies they needed to meet the demand.

He was still annoyed that she'd involved Alex Fielding in his personal business, but Nick also knew her intentions were in the right place. She cared about him. She wanted to see him happy. To her that meant with a wife and family, but that simply would not be his reality. The memory of the day his father died never left him.

Due to running the restaurant, his father hadn't been in the bleachers for his baseball games or there to pat him on the back when Nick had won the science fair thanks to his love of gastronomy. But those things had never mattered. What mattered was their time in the kitchen together. Moments when Nick had cooked a chicken marsala just right or created the perfect Bolognese sauce and Dad had beamed with pride.

He'd lived for that look. That approval. And then it was gone. Nick couldn't imagine inflicting that pain on a child of his own.

Mom was never the same either, and her new husband was nothing like the man she'd lost. Gus was quiet. Unassuming. An insurance salesman who would rather sit on the couch watching inane television than do anything else. Deep down, Nick suspected she'd only married him because she *didn't* love him.

She'd needed someone to take care of her so she'd found a man who wouldn't ask for much, who would keep her safe with a roof over her head, and who would be easier to lose when the time came. The suggestion made her sound heartless, but she was really heartbroken and found the best way to cope that she could.

Aware that he needed to bring a peace offering, Nick rang Nota's doorbell with a bowl of his homemade Tiramisu in hand. She answered the door looking more tired than usual.

"Nota, are you okay?"

She waved his concern away. "I'm fine. Just a little flare-up."

The arthritis was flaring up more and more lately. "Is the medication Fielding gave you not working?"

"It's fine." She led him into the kitchen and took a seat at the table. "Sit with me."

In front of her was a photo album just like the one

Mia had given Nick for his birthday. He had yet to open his past that first page.

"Where did this come from?" he asked, reluctant to travel down this memory lane.

"Mia made us all one." When Nick remained several feet from the table, she patted the empty spot next to her. "Sit, my boy. We need to talk."

Resigned to his fate, he slid into the scat and pushed the Tiramisu her way. "I brought you something."

She lifted the lid to see the dessert inside, then clicked it shut. "Thank you. That will be good with my coffee in the morning."

After placing the treat in the fridge, Nick returned to his seat. "So what are we talking about?"

"The family."

Tension tightened the muscles across his back. "What about them?"

Nota opened the book, ran a finger gently over the first picture, and then turned the page. There Nick saw a scattered collection of black-and-white photographs. Leaning toward the album, he spotted the year 1955 at the bottom of several of them.

"Is that you and Grandpa?"

"It is. That's the year we started dating." Pointing to the image in the top right corner of the page, she said, "This was our first date. I turned eighteen the week before and Papa finally let him take me out."

Nick looked closer and marveled at the resemblance

between father and son. The image could have easily been of his dad.

"He was three years older than you, right?"

She nodded. "We met two years before, when I was sixteen and he was nineteen. I fell in love the moment I laid eyes on him, but your Papa Karras wouldn't even consider letting me go out with a boy. Especially not one so much older."

Since he'd always felt protective of Mia, Nick understood his great-grandfather's thinking. Not that his sister had ever wanted to date a boy, older, younger, or otherwise.

"Is that him?" he asked, pointing to a picture of an older man wearing a white sleeveless undershirt and dark pants.

"Ah, yes. That's Papa. He always stood like that. Stomach out. Hands on his hips. Cigarette clenched between his teeth."

How anyone lived past thirty back then was a miracle. The men on Nota's side had nearly all lived well into their seventies, but Nick had no idea how considering their unhealthy lifestyle.

Nota turned the page to her wedding photos taken the following year. "Other than when I had your father, this was the happiest day of my life." She scanned the images with misty eyes and then scooted the book closer to Nick. "Here's Papa again. I'll never forget how he cried the whole way as he walked me down the aisle. And here's your Papa Stamatis."

Nick looked closer. "But how. I thought he died in the war."

"That was your great-grandfather. This is his father, your great-great-grandfather, Nickolai Stamatis. The man you're named after. He lived well into his seventies." She pointed to another picture. "And this is your great-uncle John, your grandfather's older brother." Nota glanced to the ceiling as she did the silent math. "He was twenty-five here, I believe. We lost him back in 2003. Such a dear man."

All of these Stamatis men living to old age was news to Nick.

"Why didn't I hear about these guys when I was growing up? I never met any great-uncles."

"Of course you did," she assured him. "You were just too young to remember."

"Nota, I was eighteen in 2003. I'd remember."

She turned the page. "John moved to California in the late eighties so you would have been very young the last time you saw him and we didn't attend the funeral." Adjusting the reading glasses on her nose, she said, "Here we are now. Your father's first baby picture." The image was in black and white and low quality, but the tuft of dark hair and disgruntled look were clearly visible. "He was the love of my life from the moment I heard his first cry."

Leaning closer, Nick saw similarities with his own baby pictures. The same unruly hair, round face, and plump cheeks. Though to be fair, that described most newborns.

"Was he a good baby?"

Chuckling, she brushed her hand over the image. "He came into the world the same way he lived the rest of his life—loudly and with great enthusiasm. I didn't sleep at all for the first year, and even the neighbors complained about the noise. That's why we bought the house. So we would stop disturbing people on the other side of those thin apartment walls."

As she continued to turn pages, Nick felt as if he were traveling through time. The clothing and hair changed with each new decade, but the faces stayed the same. There were pictures of his father and grandfather together that Nick had never seen before, and he recognized the pride in his dad's eyes whenever he stood next to his own father. The same hero worship that he'd felt as a kid.

Memories floated back as they reached the years when Nick and Mia were young. The four of them in front of the Christmas tree. Mom and Mia the day of her first communion. Dad and Nota together in the kitchen. He often said she taught him everything he knew.

They finally reached the end of the book and instead of pictures, the space was filled with a Stamatis family tree that branched out wide across two pages.

At the bottom were Nick and Mia, and the tree grew from there. What caught Nick's eye was a string of

Stamatis men on the same level as his father, all of which had birthdates but no death dates.

"Could Mia not find the details on everyone?" he asked.

"Oh, no. She got everyone for the first four generations."

Nick pointed to the four men he'd never heard of. "Who are these?"

"Those are John's sons, your father's cousins. They all stayed on the West Coast so I've only ever seen pictures of them. It would be nice to have a reunion so we could all be in the same room at least once."

"They're alive?"

She leaned back in her chair. "Yes, they are. That's why I'm showing this to you. If you won't listen to us, maybe you'll believe if you see the truth. Not all Stamatis men die young, dear boy. In fact, other than Alexander, who died in the war, your father and grandfather are the only ones who left us too soon."

Struggling to process this news, Nick stared at the names before him. According to their birthdates, they were all in their eighties and each had multiple descendants, both children and grandchildren. One, another Nickolai, even had great-grandchildren.

"I never knew," he murmured as his world shifted beneath him.

The fate he'd accepted long ago faded into something brighter. Something that allowed him to consider so many more possibilities. At the same time, the injustice of his life crystallized. The randomness of who got to live and who didn't. Of who had to lose those most important to them and who got to keep their families whole.

Nota laid her gnarled hand over his. "You have not been given a death sentence. Don't let this belief of yours keep you from fully living anymore. Please. If not for yourself, then for me. I want to see you happy before I go."

Feeling as if he'd been handed a reprieve from his worst fears, Nick looked her in the eye. "I'll do my best to try. For both of us."

10

NICK STAMATIS WAS NOT LAUREN'S FAVORITE PERSON right now. *He* was the reason she had bruises on her knees, calluses on her hands, and sweat in places she didn't want to think about.

She and Mona had survived the first course but finished second to Deborah's team. Which was humiliating considering they'd had the advantage of having only two members. The fewer members, the less time it should take, but by the time they'd crossed the fourth obstacle, Mona had received two warnings for language. The park took a strong stance to protect the ears of their younger patrons, and a third warning would have put them off the course entirely.

By the end, they'd found colorful ways to express their frustration, such as fudge bucket, mother heifer, and Lauren's new favorite, son of a dumpster fire. She was even considering posting them in the kitchen as suggested alternatives.

Despite their second place finish though, they were still in the running for the advantage since the final time would include both the first and second courses. The second was two levels up, which put them forty feet off the ground. Jackson had done his best, but had been unable to force himself up to the higher level, which left two teams with two members. Axel and Penny were both young and agile so if Mona and Lauren were going to win, they'd need to move fast.

Unfortunately, fast was not in Mona's vocabulary.

"We're so close," Lauren encouraged. "This is the last one. You can do this."

"The chairs are moving," Mona snapped.

They'd already traversed a similar obstacle below, but up here, the chairs were strung together with two feet of space between them instead of against each other like before.

"Everything is moving. The quicker you get over here, the quicker we get off this contraption. The next part is on the ground, remember?" A quick check of the competition revealed Penny crossing a giant spider web of rope while Axel waited on the other side. "We're going to lose; just get on the damn chairs!"

"Language!" came a voice over a bullhorn.

If Lauren ever found the source of those warnings, she was going to tell them exactly where they could stick that horn.

"All right. All right. I'm coming."

Mona stepped onto the first chair and Lauren said, "Faster."

The other woman stopped and glared. "Are you going to harass me all the way across because I will stay over here just to pi…" She caught herself in time. "Just to tick you off."

"Fine." Lauren leaned back against the pole. "I'll shut up."

"That would be a first," her partner mumbled.

When Mona was four chairs from the end, Lauren checked on Penny and found her struggling in the middle of the web.

"We've got a chance, Mona. We can still get that advantage."

Finding some reserve of courage, the woman bolted across the last few chairs and together they did a victory dance on the platform before zip lining back to the tower. Lauren was starting to enjoy that part. Gliding on a strap four stories off the ground did not sound like something she should enjoy, but the wind in her hair combined with the gorgeous view over the water was actually kind of soothing.

She waited for Mona to reach the center and helped her inside. They both turned to Everette, who always seemed to be wherever they landed. "Did we win?"

He wrote the time from his stopwatch down on his clipboard and looked up with a smile. "You did."

The victory dance commenced as they spun in

circles, wrapped in a sweaty hug. Separating, they high-fived and Lauren realized she hadn't touched let alone hugged another person in longer than she could remember. Well, except for Nick, but this was not the time to think about *that*.

Penny and Axel popped through another door of the tower, followed less than a minute later by Deborah and her team coming in from another direction.

"How did you like the courses?" Everette asked.

Mona growled and Lauren cut in to save the young man's life. "These were great but what's our advantage?"

"I'll tell you once we get to the hill."

"The hill?" Deborah repeated.

"Yes, ma'am. Let's get you unclipped and we can head out."

Once they were free of the belay, Lauren felt the loss of the safety cord. As they marched behind Everette down the narrow walkway, picking up Jackson on the way, she realized that she'd come to trust the safety harness.

Too bad life didn't come with one of those.

"Here we are," their guide said as they reached the beach.

Ahead of them was a steep mound of sand, at the base of which was a pool of water. Identical pools flanked the hill on both sides. At different points up the mound, objects similar to the ones on the courses were embedded in the sand, and a bright-red flag waved at the top.

"What is this?" Lauren asked.

"This is where you come together as a team. Because you and Mona had the fastest combined time on the courses, you get to be the callers."

"What are we calling?" Mona asked.

"Instructions." Pointing to the flag, he said, "The goal is to get everyone up there."

"So we're just climbing the hill?" Axel said.

"Yes, but it isn't as easy as it sounds." Everette lifted a mesh bag off a hook at the end of the walkway. "These are blindfolds. You'll all be wearing them, and it's Mona and Lauren's job to talk you up the hill, making sure you don't fall off."

Lauren stared at the hill, looking for the catch when Mona said, "Bless the Lord, we get to stay on the ground."

"Not necessarily. You and Lauren have to get to the top first, and you'll give the instructions from up there."

"Then how is this an advantage?" she asked.

"You aren't in danger of getting wet," Deborah answered.

Everette's smile widened. "Actually, they are. Though they get to climb without the blindfold, they will be attached to each of you as you work your way up. If you fall, so do they."

No wonder they were still wearing the harnesses.

Penny clapped and said, "This sounds fun."

"Not the time," Deborah snapped. "Let's get this over with."

An extra-long strap was attached to both Lauren and Mona's harness, and then a narrow bridge was laid across the bottom puddle—though puddle was an understatement. They used the various buried objects to haul themselves to the top. Lauren had no idea how the order was decided, but Axel was attached to Mona's cord first, then blindfolded, led over the bridge, and helped onto the base of the hill. The bridge was then removed and Everette yelled for them to start.

Lauren spoke first. "Take three steps up and reach out for the barrel!"

"What the hell are you doing?" Mona asked. "If I'm the one who gets wet if he falls, then I'm the one who gets to give the orders."

"We're both supposed to get them up here," Lauren argued. The woman was more likely to cuss her teammates out than to have enough patience to guide them all the way up.

"It is not going to kill you to let someone else take the lead for once. This is supposed to be team building. So trust your teammate."

Attempting to embrace the experience, she held her hands up in surrender. "Fine. But keep him close to the center and don't forget to describe exactly what he should be reaching for."

"Woman, I will throw you off this damn hill. You are seriously testing how badly I want this job."

Lauren clamped her mouth shut. So much for any bonding they'd done on the course.

Less than a minute later, Axel joined them at the top, and the team below cheered the victory. Brit went next, attached to Lauren's tether. She too made the journey with little trouble, and they progressed through the rest of the process until Jackson remained at the bottom alone.

Everette attached him to Lauren with a click and yelled up, "He's all yours."

As she kneeled on the hard sand, Lauren's palms began to sweat. Jackson was the largest of the group, outweighing her by at least a hundred pounds. He was also the oldest, and with his fear of heights, was going to be the most difficult to get to the top.

"Focus on my voice," she said. "Take one step to your right, and then start climbing. I'll tell you when you get close to the barrel." Jackson did as ordered. "Okay, less than a foot up from your right hand is the top of the barrel. Slowly reach up until you can feel it."

As he extended his arm, sand fell out from under his left foot and he slid down. Lauren nearly went flying when Mona yelled, "Grab her!"

Strong arms wrapped around her middle, knocking the breath from her lungs but keeping her on the hill.

"Are we allowed to do this?" Axel said.

Lauren turned to see him holding Mona and Deborah holding him.

She looked down the hill, expecting to hear Everette tell them to let go, but he remained silent. So it was by any means necessary. All righty then.

"We've got this, guys. Just don't let go." To Jackson she yelled, "You're doing great, buddy. Get your footing and try again."

He did so and when his hand gripped the barrel, Lauren let out the breath she didn't realized she was holding.

"Good job. Pull yourself up and once you feel yourself get level with the barrel, you should be able to reach the chair arm on your left."

When his hips were even with the barrel, his left arm flailed about, finding nothing but air.

Lauren was pulled forward again, and Mona's arms tightened. She patted the woman's wrist. "I need to breathe."

"You want to breathe or you want to live?"

If she hadn't been in such a precarious position, Lauren would have laughed at the contradictory question.

"Slow movements, Jackson," she called. "Come up a little higher. There you go. Okay, the handle is right there."

His hand connected with wood and his head dropped with relief, but they still had another fifteen feet to go. This is where the objects spread out more so she had to decide whether to keep him in the middle, trusting his ability to climb without the handholds, or chance sending him closer to the edge to find assistance.

Deciding he would be the best judge, she said,

"Jackson, do you think you can climb up using just the sand?"

After a brief hesitation, he said, "I can try."

The man was the definition of a team player. "I need you to be certain. It's okay if you need the extra help to pull yourself up. I just need to know what will work best for you."

"I need the help," he replied. "There's a metal ring somewhere close, isn't there?"

He must have studied the course while everyone else went up.

"Yes. It's about two feet above you, but nearly three feet to your left." Dropping his belly to the sand, he pushed up and slid sideways, using the barrel as a step. "That's good. You're almost there."

Strong fingers touched metal and he yelled, "I've got it!"

She talked him past two more objects to reach the most difficult section where the remaining items had been embedded much farther apart. A wooden post jutted out of the sand on his right, but was perilously close to the edge, while the small tire on his left was farther away from his current position. Without something to keep his feet planted, Jackson could easily tumble down the hill, taking the rest of them down with him.

"I need you to move very slowly through this next part," she said, keeping her voice as calm as possible. "There's a peg on your right."

"It's too far out," Dodge whispered. "Send him the other way."

Lauren shook her head. "He can do this." Raising her voice, she said, "Push yourself up a little higher, and crawl your fingers over the sand up and to your right."

Despite his best efforts, the post was still far out of reach.

"Change to put your left foot on the plank so you can scoot more to the right."

"I can't watch," Penny said.

"No, I think she's right," Deborah said. "If he takes his time, he can do this."

Jackson set his forehead on the sand as he edged his right foot off the support and quickly switched to his left. He then flopped once more, extending his right arm as far as he could. A second later his fingers grazed the post, but missed, sending his body weight hurling toward the edge.

"Come back!" Lauren screamed. Mona cursed up a blue streak but held on tight.

Jackson caught himself, lying still except for his head lulling back and forth on the sand. "I'm not going to make it."

Lauren refused to give up on him. "Yes, you are. Stay right there and run your right hand across the sand to the left. That's right. Slowly. You're so close." His hand found the peg and this time took hold. "That's it. Now pull up and you'll feel another peg just above your left hand."

Jackson pulled himself up between the two pegs and Lauren scooted sideways to get closer to him.

"What are you doing?" Mona said, panic in her voice.

"We have to reach him. Lower me down a little bit. Everyone hold on to the person in front of you and whatever you do, do not let go."

Picking up on the closeness of her voice, Jackson said, "I'm almost there, aren't I?"

"Yes." She reached out her hand, ignoring the tiny pebbles digging into her knees. "Take my hand." She smacked her palm on the sand to help him locate it. "Keep stretching. We can do this."

Moments that felt like hours passed before they finally made contact.

"That's it." With a strength she didn't know she had, Lauren yanked hard and yelled, "Pull, everyone!"

In an instant, Lauren was on her back, Jackson's hand still in hers and the others were leaping for joy around them. She worked to fill her lungs and could have cried with relief. She'd done it. They'd all done it.

Deborah and Brit helped Lauren to her feet while Axel got Jackson off the ground. High fives were exchanged before Mona said, "Well, shit. Now how do we get down?"

Ignoring the profanity, Everette called up, "Turn around." They spun as one to find a giant, inflatable slide coming off the other side of the hill. "Grab hands and take a leap," he said.

Pilar's kitchen staff exchanged uncertain looks

before Lauren held out both hands. "You heard him. Let's get the hell off this hill." Hands were joined and when they were all at the edge, she said, "On the count of three. One, two, three!"

Lauren jumped, landing on her bottom, and laughed all the way down the slide.

11

Nick had just removed the chicken from the oven when, as promised, Lauren arrived on his threshold, six-pack in hand, at exactly ten o'clock. She wore leggings, an oversized hoodie, and Vans—all black. Her platinum hair was in a short ponytail at the base of her skull and her nose was badly sunburned.

"Tough day?" he asked, taking the beer and stepping aside for her to enter.

"I didn't like you very much this morning," she said in reply. "That place is way scarier than I imagined."

"You're here so I guess you aren't holding a grudge." He walked past her, adding, "The food will be ready in a few minutes. Go ahead and have a seat at the table." She did so, settling gently into the chair. "Are you okay?" he asked, fearing she'd really hurt herself.

"My body aches in places I didn't know I had." She

slowly relaxed. "I thought I was in good shape, but I was wrong."

"Have you taken anything for the pain?"

"I don't have anything on hand and didn't make it to the store before it closed."

Nick opened a cabinet next to the fridge and pulled out a bottle of pain pills. Popping the cap on his way to the table, he said, "Here." She held her palm up, revealing nasty blisters. "Did you wear gloves?"

"Obviously not, but Jackson's hands look worse than mine."

Real worry set in. "Let me dish up this chicken, and then I want to hear the whole story."

Two minutes later, the plates were on the table, along with silverware, napkins, and two beers.

"I know I brought the beer, but if I have that, you're going to have to scrape me off the floor. Can I have a soda?"

"Sure." Nick retrieved the drink and returned to his seat.

Lauren examined the food with her fork. "Is this stuffed chicken Valentino?"

"Yes, ma'am. So what happened today?"

She struggled to cut her chicken with the sore fingers and Nick took pity on her. Reaching across the table, he cut the food for her.

In a moment of obvious weakness, she said, "That might be the sweetest thing anyone's ever done for me." Sliding the first bite between her lips, she chewed twice and stopped. "Holy crap. Dis is awesome," she said around the food.

"I'm glad you like it. Now back to today." The suspense was killing him. "Did you leave there a cohesive team or are you about to be running that kitchen by yourself?"

She loaded up her fork with another bite. "This is where you get to say I told you so. It absolutely worked. I mean, we were barely tolerating each other for the first hour, but they made us do this hill thing. Mona and I were at the top and everyone else was blindfolded. We had to talk them up the hill past all of these buried obstacles."

"The tether test," he replied.

"You've done it?" Lauren asked, stopping with the fork halfway to her mouth. "Dude. That shit was scary. Jackson went last and he almost took both of us over the side, but Mona grabbed me and everyone else jumped on to create some human lifeline. I still can't believe we didn't end up in the water."

He'd never seen her so animated. "I've only ever watched others do it, but it sounds like you guys figured it out." Pointing out the obvious, he said, "So you learned to trust them."

Blue eyes went wide. "I didn't say that."

The woman had entirely missed the point. "You just said the team formed a lifeline. What happened after they did that?"

"I scooted down the hill until Jackson could reach my hand, and then we pulled him up."

"So you *trusted* them to keep you safe while you gave someone else a reason to trust you."

The old cliché of a light bulb going off over someone's head came to life in that moment. Every thought rolled across her face, from denial to acceptance and about three steps in between.

"I trusted them," she mumbled, speaking more to herself than to him.

Nick held his tongue while she processed the revelation. He'd had one of his own earlier in the day and understood how off-balance she must have felt. Though he also wondered why she'd been so distrusting in the first place. He knew his own reasons for his faulty thinking, but in Lauren's case, the causes were likely more traumatic. No one was born refusing to trust people.

"Are you glad you went then?"

"I am."

"You're from Boston, right?" He knew the answer but wanted to get her talking again.

"Worcester, technically, but the Boston area."

Reaching for his beer, he asked, "What made you want to be a chef?"

Lauren moved a piece of chicken around on her plate. "Mom had to work a lot, so I had to take care of Knox. That's my younger brother," she added. "He's in the Army now. At some point I got tired of chicken nuggets and mac and cheese so when a neighbor tossed some cookbooks out by the dumpster, I swiped them."

"How old were you?"

"Nine, maybe. That's when I made my first full meal, which came out of a box, but considering I'd had to stand on a stool just to reach the faucet, I felt pretty accomplished."

Nick tried to imagine what it would have been like to be responsible for Mia at such a young age and couldn't even picture how that would have gone. Though Dad had put him in the kitchen pretty early, he'd not been cooking anything solo before fourteen or fifteen years old, and even then not without adult supervision.

"Where was your dad?"

She put her fork down. "I never knew my dad. Neither did Knox. They weren't the same guy." Messing with the string on her hoodie, she said, "How did you end up on Anchor Island?"

Accepting the change of subject, he said, "Mia and I moved here to take care of Nota. She visited for a vacation years ago and fell in love with the place. Within six months she'd made it her home, but then a couple years ago she fell and broke her hip. We decided she needed family around, so here we are."

"Where were you before?"

"North Jersey. As you know, life in a busy kitchen gets old. After fifteen years, I'd had enough, so getting word the spot was open at Dempsey's made the decision an easy one."

Lauren watched him closely. "You don't regret it? This island must get boring after a while."

"Have you been bored yet?" he asked.

"I've only been here for five weeks, and those have been spent trying to get this restaurant where I want it."

Asking a leading question, he said, "Did you go out much back in Boston?"

"Working eighties hours a week doesn't leave much time for a social life."

"But you weren't bored?"

Getting his point, her lips curled into a half smile and some of the earlier light returned to her eyes. "You like to be right, don't you?"

"Don't you?" he returned.

"I think you know the answer to that."

Nick reached for his beer. "Yes, I do. Your food is getting cold over there."

Eyes on her plate, she said, "Do you mind if I take this home for later? I don't feel like eating right now."

Sensing he'd crossed a line, he said, "I'm sorry that I brought up your family. I didn't mean to pry."

Lauren shook her head with a resigned expression. "I don't like to talk about the past, that's all."

"Not a problem." Rising to his feet, Nick picked up both of their plates.

"You aren't done yet," she said, reaching to tug her plate back. "Go ahead and finish."

He would not sit there and eat in front of her,

especially when he'd been the one to send her appetite packing.

"It's fine. Go ahead and sit on the couch while I clean this up."

"I can help." She hopped up and immediately groaned.

Chuckling, he carried the plates to the counter. "Like I said, have a seat on the couch. This won't take long."

He slid her food into a glass bowl and clicked on the lid as she asked, "What's this?"

Nick glanced over to see her looking at the photo album on the coffee table. "Mia made that for me for my birthday. A kind of our-family-through-the-years thing."

After his lunch with Nota, Nick had finally taken the time to flip through it. His collection contained more pictures from their childhood, showing that Mia had personalized the books according to who they were for. He assumed her own looked much like his.

"Can I look at it?" Lauren asked.

"Sure." Once the leftovers were in the fridge, Nick joined her on the couch. "That's my dad," he said as she examined a picture taken in front of the restaurant.

"Is that you beside him?"

"That's me." Knowing what she was thinking, he said, "I was going through a chubby phase."

Her laughter was all the better for how rarely she shared it. "You were just big-boned," she said, trying to be kind.

"I believe husky was the word on my jeans."

Lauren turned the page. "Mia hasn't changed a bit. How old is she here?"

Nick had to look closer. "I'd say about twelve. That's when she got her braces and started smiling like she was trying to hide a hamster in her mouth."

"Spoken like a mean big brother." She scanned the next page, smacked a finger on one picture in particular, and cut her eyes his way. "A white tuxedo?"

"I was fourteen and Lorinda Witherspoon, my date to that dance, picked it out."

"Then I am judging Lorinda and her middle school taste."

She turned the page again and caught a blister on the corner. "Ouch." The damaged digit shot into her mouth.

"We need to put something on those."

As he lifted off the couch, she tried to argue that she was fine, but couldn't speak clearly for the finger between her lips. Nick ignored her and proceeded to the bathroom to snag petroleum jelly from his medicine cabinet, but he couldn't find the bandages. He'd recently used the last in a box, but he was certain he'd bought another when the first had gotten low. The hunt took longer than he'd planned, but he finally found the full box under the sink.

"Here we go," he said, returning to the living room to find Lauren slumped over and sound asleep.

Leaving the first aid items on the kitchen counter, he grabbed a blanket off his bed, lifted her feet onto the couch so she wasn't twisted at an odd angle, and then tucked her in. This was not how he'd planned to end the night, but she was in this condition thanks to his suggestion, so he only had himself to blame.

Collecting the items off the counter, he went to work on her hands.

———

LAUREN HEARD a distant voice calling her name and fought to drag herself out of the darkness. Shifting to stretch her limbs, she moaned in pain and opened one eye. The small effort was for naught since wherever she was, the room was pitch-black.

"Come on, sleepyhead. We need to get moving."

Brain finally starting to function, she recognized the voice. And immediately panicked.

Jerking upright, she looked around, ignoring her screaming muscles.

"Hello?" she said.

"Over here." Following the sound, she found Nick in the chair at the end of the coffee table, the glow from his cell phone screen lighting his face. "How do you feel?"

"Like I've been hit by a truck. What happened?"

His sexy laugh should not have been so arousing in her half-conscious state.

"You passed out so I let you sleep. The pain pills are on the table in front of you next to a bottle of water. I put a fresh toothbrush on the bathroom sink, and you're welcome to use anything else you need."

The pills were a must, but the rest she'd take care of at home. "You should have woken me up and sent me home." Pulling the band from her hair, she scratched her scalp, counting on the darkness to hide how awful she must look.

"You were exhausted. You didn't even wake up when I put the ointment on your hands."

Lauren flexed her fingers and felt the Band-Aids for the first time. "Why would you do that?"

Nick's phone light went off. "They'll be worse if they dry out. We pull out in ten minutes. Do you need help getting up?"

Pull out? "You don't need to drive me home. I can walk."

"You aren't going home. We're going to get some fish."

Fishing? The man expected her to go fishing with hands full of blisters and a body she could barely move? All Lauren wanted was a hot bath and a soft bed. The man could go fishing all by himself.

"There's no way." Lauren pushed herself off the couch and the agony nearly sent her back down. She wavered but Nick caught her before she could crumble. Shoving him off, she said, "I can stand on my own."

He held on despite her efforts. "If I let go, you'll be in a heap on the floor in seconds. Just give yourself a minute."

Pride made her want to push him away even harder, but Nick was right. Her legs were like overcooked noodles and her head was spinning.

"You didn't eat enough last night. I've got a protein smoothie in the fridge. You can have that until we get some solid food into you."

Lauren couldn't remember the last time someone took care of her like this. Or if anyone ever had. She'd never considered curling into another human being, but that's all she wanted to do in that moment. Tuck herself against Nick and let him carry the weight of the world for a while.

Instead, she took several deep breaths, allowing her mind to come fully awake and her legs to steady.

"Thank you," she mumbled, loosening the grip she had on his sleeve. "I'm not used to leaning on people."

"I can tell." Loosening his hold around her waist, he said, "Better?"

"Yeah." She tested her legs and was relieved when they held her up. "I can make it home."

"If you insist on going home, I'll drive you, but you'll be missing out."

Her experience with fishing was limited to a summer in her childhood when one of her mom's boyfriends— possibly the only one who had ever shown any interest in her children—had taken Lauren and Knox out to a lake and taught them how to bait their own hooks. In the evening, they'd cooked what they'd caught and her love of cooking over an open flame had been born.

She hadn't touched a pole since and was in no shape to do so today.

"I can't go fishing, Nick. I'll be lucky if I can hold my knives at work."

"I didn't say we were *going* fishing. We're going to pick up some fresh fish. No poles involved."

Lauren looked over to the sliding glass doors and saw nothing but moonlight glinting off the water. "Where are we going to find fresh fish in the middle of the night?"

"It's six a.m. The sun will be up soon. And we're surrounded by fresh fish, remember? We're on an island." He thought he was so cute. "Are you in or not?"

He had her curious now. "Which way is the bathroom?"

Nick took her by the shoulders and turned her to the right. "Walk straight ahead. I'll have the smoothie waiting when you come back."

Careful not to trip, she staggered across the room, hands outstretched to find the bathroom doorway. Once inside, she patted around for the switch and Nick called, "It's on the left." So he was a chef, a nurse, and a psychic. Was there anything the man couldn't do?

Maybe if she hadn't fallen asleep, Lauren would have discovered more of his talents. Then again, considering her current condition, it's likely her body would have cramped up at an inopportune time and humiliated her much more than she already was.

Locating the switch, she flipped the light on and nearly blinded herself. "Motherfu—"

"You good?" called Nick.

"Sure," she called back. "All good."

Lauren closed the door, paused to let her eyes adjust, and then quickly took care of the necessities. Minutes later, she exited the bathroom feeling presentable if not totally human. Pretending that every step didn't hurt was difficult, but she did her best not to whimper as she returned to the kitchen.

"Pills first," Nick said, nodding toward the bottle he'd moved to the island counter. "You can drink the smoothie on the way." Next to the medicine was water and a tall, slim bottle with green liquid inside. She tried to sniff the concoction through the straw. "It tastes better than it looks," he said.

Her stomach growled and she decided to take his word for it. The pills went down with ease and would hopefully kick in fast.

"I'm ready."

Nick grabbed a set of keys from a bowl on the counter. "Then let's go."

12

NICK PARKED HIS TRUCK BESIDE PILAR'S AT THE ENTRANCE to the pier as dawn broke over the horizon. Muted orange and yellow streaks danced across the sky like a painting hanging over the water and signaling that the sun would rise from the salty depths any minute. With a deep breath he filled his lungs with fresh sea air, one of his favorite perks about living on the island.

Lauren had powered through the smoothie before they'd gotten halfway through the village, and as he'd expected, she'd guessed his secret ingredient for making the shakes more tolerable—date syrup. To her credit, she didn't ask many questions once they arrived, content to follow as he took a right and headed toward a fishing boat at the far end of the docks.

"Morning, Wyatt," he called as they grew closer.

"Morning, Nick. Who's that you've got with ye?"

"This is Lauren Riley. She's the new chef at Pilar's

here." He pointed to the building behind them. "What used to be the Marina restaurant."

The older man smiled to reveal the wide gap between his two front teeth. "Does that mean you're bringing me new business?" he asked, his heavy Welsh accent cutting out several syllables.

Nick looked to Lauren and her eyes went wide. "Sure?" she said.

"Delivery will be easy." Wyatt lifted a large bucket out of the boat and onto the dock as if it weighed no more than a sack of flour. "Got some good-sized mahi, along with both blackfin and yellowfin." Another bucket came over the side. "And plenty of flounder."

Lauren stepped closer to the second bucket. "Fresh flounder?"

"Yes, ma'am. Nothing better."

Like a kid in a candy store, she examined the offerings with her nose nearly in the buckets. "You can supply these on a regular basis?" she asked.

"Year-round," Wyatt replied. "We take Sundays and Mondays off, but we hit the water the rest of the week."

"This is amazing," she said to Nick. "I could make countless dishes with these."

"We're only making one this morning." He joined her to examine the flounder. Drawing one out, he said, "We'll take this and you can send the regular amount over to Dempsey's."

"Consider it done. And you can have that one on the

house," Wyatt added. "An introductory offer for the new chef."

The fish was bagged in ice and after a brief goodbye, they headed back to Nick's place. Lauren appeared more awake and walked into the house without hobbling, revealing a quick recovery from the day before. Nick tossed the packaged fish onto the counter and opened the pantry to gather what he needed. Turning, he found Lauren sitting at the kitchen table.

"What are you doing?" he asked, setting the salt, paprika, and black pepper on the counter.

"I assume you're making breakfast so I'm staying out of your way."

"*We* are making breakfast. Flounder and eggs to be exact." He pulled an apron from a drawer and tossed it her way. "Suit up."

Lauren leaned back in her chair. "You expect me to cook with you in that tiny kitchen?"

Though small, he'd long ago created a setup that was more than adequate for anything he wanted to make. The lack of space just meant they might bump into each other now and then, and he had no problem with that.

Nick pressed his hands to the island counter. "Are you insulting the size of my kitchen?"

Her attempt to hold in the laughter failed but she recovered quickly. "You have to admit. There isn't much room in there."

Holding her gaze, he said, "What's the matter, Riley. You too intimidated to cook with me?"

Blue eyes narrowed and he knew he'd pushed the right button. Rising from the table and putting on the apron, she said, "Where are the knives?"

"Top right drawer." He retrieved the remaining ingredients from the fridge and placed the scallions, parsley, and capers next to the butcher block. "You chop while I clean the fish."

As if out of habit, she said, "Yes, Chef."

She opened the drawer and Nick reached around her for the tools he needed. Leaning close to her ear, he said, "We're just two people making breakfast, Lauren. Call me Nick."

Her body pressed back against his. "I can do that."

The temptation to delay the meal for other activities was hard to resist, but after his talk with Nota, Nick had decided to take this slow. Years of meaningless encounters had left him wanting more. Whether Lauren was the woman for him was yet to be seen, but he didn't just desire her. He liked her. The confidence. The ambition. The vulnerability she fought so hard to hide. Accepting that she'd needed help with the staff had not come easy for her, but she'd come to his door, which said she was starting to trust him.

A development she likely didn't even realize, and he wasn't about to point out. Not yet.

Nick stepped away, ignoring the demands from his body to do otherwise. "I've got a cleaning station outside. If you need anything while I'm out there, feel free to search around."

"Um...okay." She picked a knife and reached for the scallions. "I'll be fine."

Fish in hand, he retreated through the sliding glass door, grateful for the cool breeze coming off the water. Lucky for him, cleaning a fish was the unsexiest thing Nick could think of, and by the time he returned inside, the urge to strip Lauren out of her hoodie was gone.

Mostly.

———

"THIS WAS BETTER THAN I EXPECTED," she said, eating the last bite of fish before shoving her plate away.

Nick's mixed signals had kept Lauren in a state of confusion throughout the cooking. One minute he'd be reaching around her, their bodies making contact that lit tiny fires in her bloodstream whenever they touched. The next he'd dance away, acting as if nothing had happened. Lucky for him, the meal had been worth the frustration.

Lauren still felt like a live wire, but at least she'd been satisfied in one way.

"So what's the plan for today?" Nick asked, dropping his napkin atop his empty plate.

"On the trip back from Nag's Head, I let everyone know to come in at nine." She checked the clock above his pantry door to see she had just over an hour. "We'll begin working on the dishes I'd like to put on the menu."

Crossing his arms on the table, he asked, "What have you come up with?"

She reached for her phone and pulled up her Notes app. "This is what I'm shooting for."

Dark brows arched high. "That was easier than I expected."

"What was easier?"

"You showing me your menu. I thought you might say it was none of my business."

She would have at the start of the week, and that smirk on his face said he knew it. "Unless you plan to add pistachio crusted pork loin, a noodle bowl, or roasted vegetables with Pappardell to the Dempsey's menu, I think I'm safe."

Nick perused her list in silence. While making breakfast, he'd cooked with precision, skill, and efficiency, proving that he was much more than a bar food cook. The fish had been perfectly cleaned, and he'd tossed in the seasonings by eye, tasting as he went. He'd let her taste as well and listened when she shared her opinion.

A rare occurrence in her experience.

Lauren hovered on the edge of her seat, not entirely comfortable with how much she wanted his approval. When he pursed his lips but remained quiet, she forced herself to look away in an attempt to pretend that his response didn't matter.

"Looks good," he finally said, allowing her to once again

take a full breath. "You're smart to go heavy on the seafood, for obvious reasons, and though at first glance the dishes seem simple, they're actually quite complex. You said you'd offer a more refined dining experience, and based on this, you've found a way to do that without being pretentious."

Unsure if the last bit was a compliment or not, she said, "You thought my food would be pretentious?"

"I think fine dining is pretentious," he corrected. Returning her phone, he added, "This menu is not."

Encouraged, she closed the app and set the cell back on the table. "What kind of food did your family restaurant serve?"

When they'd first met, he said he'd never attended culinary school, but instead he'd learned on the job. Finesse in the kitchen came with practice, but Nick's technique was as good as any chef she'd ever worked with. Most of whom possessed hard-earned degrees.

"Dad served traditional Greek food."

That explained his understanding of flavor. "I should have guessed."

"Yeah, the name is a dead giveaway. I could make spanakopita before I could spell it."

She longed for that kind of heritage. "Must be nice to know where you come from."

"You don't know your family's history?"

Lauren wished. "I looked up the name Riley once. Most likely Mom's ancestors worked to clear rye fields or something in the UK. Maybe they owned the fields, but I doubt it." She shrugged. "I don't know my biological father's name."

Brow furrowed, Nick leaned forward. "Your mom never told you?" When Lauren shook her head, he said, "Why don't you ask her?"

Clearing the lump in her throat, she replied, "Mom died of cancer six months ago."

He sat up straight again. "I'm so sorry."

"It's fine," she lied. "When I was young, she said my father wanted nothing to do with me, and by the time I was a teenager, I decided I wanted nothing to do with him."

"You still deserve to know who he is. What about your grandparents? Are they still alive? Could they tell you?"

Lauren had let go of having any family connections a long time ago. "They weren't in our lives either. Mom's parents didn't approve of her choice to have kids with having a husband. Mom said they were really strict and when she refused to get married just because she was pregnant, they cut her off."

A warm hand caressed her joined ones. "You know that wasn't your fault, right?"

She jerked her chin up, meeting his gaze. "What?"

"You think that if you hadn't come along, your mother's life would have been different."

No one had ever guessed how she really felt. In the rare moments when she'd shared these details, the other person had always focused on her grandparents' selfishness or her mother's mistakes. But Nick saw her truth.

"How do you know that?" Lauren whispered.

"The way you talk about her with regret instead of judgment. I get the impression that you had a difficult childhood. Most people would blame the adult in charge for that, but you don't seem to."

Difficult was an understatement but she didn't correct him. "She did the best she could with the hand she was dealt."

"A hand she dealt herself, yet you haven't blamed her for giving her parents a reason to toss her out, or for picking the wrong man to be your father."

Lauren swiped at a tear she didn't realize had fallen. "Mom picked *a lot* of wrong men, but she didn't have a whole lot of options. With two kids to feed and no diploma, good jobs were hard to come by, and two incomes were better than one." Eyes on her hands, she added, "She paid for her mistakes. Blaming her won't change anything now."

"You know none of that is your fault," Nick assured her. "It sounds like she was a victim of circumstance and some really shitty parents. Neither of which you had anything to do with."

Easy for him to say. If Lauren didn't exist, maybe Mom would have finished college and had a normal life like everyone else. Instead she lived hand to mouth, endured abusive men to keep a roof over their heads, and died at a young age because she didn't have access to the health care she so badly needed. Care that might have found the cancer early enough for her to beat it.

"I feel like I should be sitting on the couch for this." She used her napkin to dry her cheeks, unable to recall the last time she'd cried in front of anyone. "Do you charge by the hour or is the first session free?"

Collecting the empty plates, he rose to his feet. "If it'll make you feel better, I'll tell you how I resent my mother for remarrying after Dad died."

She laughed at the confession. "Do you really?"

"Yep," he said, placing the dishes in the sink. "I was nineteen and I should have been happy for her, but all I could think was that she was cheating on Dad."

Lauren carried their empty glasses into the kitchen. "Is he a good guy?"

"Gus? He's all right. Sells insurance in Florida. Dull as a butter knife, but he takes good care of her and she seems to like it down there."

Mom probably would have liked Florida. She always hated the New England winters.

"Hey," Nick said, dragging Lauren out of her thoughts. "I have to work tonight, but I'm off tomorrow."

Aware that he hadn't actually asked to see her, Lauren said, "We open in a week so I'll be working tomorrow."

Nick pulled her into his arms. "All day?"

"Why?" she said, slipping her hands around his rib cage. "Is there something I need to make time for?"

After placing a kiss on her forehead, he said, "I'd like to see you again."

He'd certainly waited long enough to make a move. "That could be arranged. Are you offering to cook for me again?"

Dark eyes cut to the ceiling as if he was pondering the question, and then he said, "Nope. It's your turn to cook for me."

That was a bold statement. "*I'm* cooking?"

"I've cooked twice already."

"I helped with breakfast," she pointed out.

"Yes, but in my kitchen on my dish. I want to see what you can cook up on your own."

She was trying to cook up something that had nothing to do with the kitchen. Rising on her toes, she brushed her lips across his. "Any requests?"

He kissed her back and said, "Surprise me."

That she could do.

Adding a purr to her voice, Lauren whispered, "Yes, Chef," and kissed him once more, enjoying the way his arms tightened when their tongues met. He was warm and solid and exactly what she needed to end her sexual drought.

When her hands slid up his chest, Nick caught them and pulled away. "You have to go to work, remember?"

Lauren checked the clock to see they had nearly forty minutes. "We could be quick."

Slowly shaking his head, he put more space between them. "When I get you into bed, I plan to take my time."

How was she supposed to argue with that?

Accepting the rain check, she returned to the table to retrieve her phone. "Tomorrow then. How about seven?" She needed time to pick up the ingredients and have a meal ready before he got there. She would also need to shower and take care of other necessities if this dinner was ending the way she hoped.

"Seven works for me."

Crossing the living room, she said, "Be prepared for an amazing meal."

Nick followed her to the door. "I'm looking forward to it."

Before leaving, she tried one more time. "Are you sure we don't have time—"

"I'm sure. Go home before I change my mind and your cooks wonder where their fearless leader is."

Why hadn't she picked a noon start time?

"Fine, but this better be worth the wait."

She was nearly over the threshold when Nick pulled her back and kissed her senseless against his front door. By the time he broke contact, his hands still warm on her heated cheeks, Lauren was a wilting mess.

"I guarantee it," he whispered against her temple.

Still dazed, she could do little more than nod as he stepped back and let her leave. Whatever she decided to cook needed to be good if it was going to be a warm-up for more of that.

13

Nick stood on the porch of Lauren's cottage, feeling like a teenager picking up his crush for their first date. For him, it might as well have been exactly that. He hadn't let himself even consider the idea of pursuing a relationship in fifteen years. Whenever he'd felt himself getting attached, he'd cut the other person loose. Not that he left a string of broken hearts in his wake.

He'd always been up front with women, and he gravitated toward the ones who felt the same way he did. No strings. Nothing serious. Lauren fell into that category so he was probably setting himself up for disappointment, but Nick wasn't looking to walk down the aisle anytime soon.

Just entertaining the idea was giving him cold sweats, yet made him excited for the future in a way he hadn't allowed himself in a long time. Would Lauren consider changing the stakes? Nick didn't know her well enough to guess. But she had let him see her vulnerable, which was a start.

Lauren needed someone who could show her what she truly deserved, and Nick needed practice being needed. If nothing else, they might both come out of this with more than when they went in.

"Knock, knock," he called through the old-fashioned screen door. Leaning close, he caught the smell of roasted garlic and his mouth watered. "Hello?"

"I'm here," she said, shuffling into the living room and pushing the door open. "Come tell me if this puree needs more salt."

Lauren strolled back into the kitchen, but Nick remained just inside the door, struck dumb by the gorgeous creature who'd just greeted him. The jeans hugged her curves like a second skin, and the loose white button-down was thin enough to reveal the black tank beneath. Her hair was down and...fluffier. Nick couldn't think of another word to describe it. She looked as if she'd just rolled out of bed after doing more than sleeping.

All he could think was that he wanted to be the reason she looked that way.

"Nick?" she said, returning to the doorway between the living room and kitchen. "Are you coming?"

His inner twelve-year-old had a response to that but Nick managed to keep him quiet.

"I am."

He joined her in the kitchen and an overload of

delicious smells assailed him. Garlic, fennel, and red wine, plus a few others he couldn't pin down. When Nick stepped up behind her at the counter, intending to drop a kiss on her neck, Lauren spun with a spoon in her hand.

"Taste this."

Before he could react, the puree hit his tongue. "Potato and...?"

"Celery root," she replied. "Does it need more salt? I can't tell. I tasted so many different dishes today that my taste buds are on overload."

"No, it's just right." Where did she find celery root at this time of year? "How did you—"

A timer went off and Lauren slid away to reach for a red-and-white oven mitt. "Perfect timing," she said, pulling a pan of Brussels sprouts from the oven. She sniffed deeply over the pan before setting it on a tea towel. "I hope you like garlic because it's my favorite thing ever and I like a lot of it on my food."

You could never have too much garlic.

"I'm good with that."

Lauren grabbed two tall glasses. "This place didn't come with wineglasses so I hope this works."

He wasn't picky about his glassware. "They'll be fine."

"Great." She shoved the glasses into his hands. "Then put these on the table and grab some silverware from that last drawer over there. I'll get this dished up and be right in."

If Nick didn't know any better, he'd think the

woman was in a hurry. "Is there a race I don't know about?"

"I just want to eat before it gets cold." She planted a quick kiss on his lips before adding, "And then we can get on with our night."

The brow wiggle made him laugh. So they *were* on the same page. Somewhat.

"I'll have the table set and be ready when you are."

Giving him a pat on the ass as he walked away, she said, "That's the spirit."

Though he'd like to think the idea of sex with him had put her in such a good mood, Nick guessed things must also be going well at the restaurant. He was still pouring the wine she'd already put on the table when Lauren breezed in, plates in hand.

"Dinner is served," she announced. "We have tuna steaks with a red wine sauce, the celery root-potato puree you already tasted, and roasted Brussels sprouts in garlic." She set the large platter on the table. "Let me grab the napkins and we'll be set."

Dashing back to the kitchen, she returned almost at a run and Nick caught her by the hand.

"You can slow down. We have all night."

Blushing, she toyed with a button on his shirt. "This is your fault. I've been thinking about this for two days."

Teasing, he said, "And yet you put garlic in the food."

As the realization dawned, her eyes went wide. "I didn't even think of that."

Nick nuzzled her ear. "If you have mouthwash, we'll be fine."

She leaned her head to the side, offering him better access to her soft skin. "I have a whole bottle." When his lips trailed down to the top of her shoulder, she murmured, "Or we can eat after."

He couldn't help but smile. "We both know these Brussels sprouts won't be good if we leave them here." Putting space between them, Nick said, "Let's eat."

Her sigh of disappointment was appreciated as they took their seats. The amazing smell had not prepared him for the rush of flavor that hit his taste buds. The fish was perfectly seasoned, the balance of acid to sweet spot-on. Lauren knew how to make a protein the star of the dish while choosing complimentary sides that both enhanced the plate and elevated the overall taste.

"Tell me you're putting this on your menu."

"I'll consider it, but I made this specifically for you."

He stopped in mid cut. "For me?"

Lauren reached for her wine. "Ever since I was a kid, I've had this weird way of knowing what food a person will like. At age six I knew my mom's favorite way to have eggs without her telling me, and on the rare occasions that we got to eat out, I always ordered for my brother and just knew what he'd want." After taking a sip, she added, "I didn't think anything of it until I went to culinary school and got to cook for other people. I could look at them and know what to make."

Nick looked at his plate and realized he'd never had

this combination before, yet every bite felt familiar. Almost comforting.

"So you're a fairy godmother chef?"

"Joke all you want, but you're already thinking about how often you can have this dish."

She wasn't wrong. "Do you picture the specific dish or just the flavors and create something from there?"

"The flavors, mostly. Like I knew you'd enjoy something warm and comfortable but with a lighter protein and a rich base. Put those ideas together and voila, you get this meal."

"That's a gift," he said. "And what cooking is all about. Giving people something that makes them happy on a plate."

Lauren looked both proud and embarrassed. "That's what my mentor said when he sponsored me for Le Cordon Bleu. They have a scholarship program and if he hadn't told me about it, I never would have even applied. As a poor kid from Worcester who'd worked her way up through the line, I never thought they'd let me in." With a head tilt, she said, "Did you ever think of going to culinary school?"

A subject he preferred to avoid, since he wasn't proud of his answer. "I didn't. Dad had me in the kitchen as soon as I was tall enough to stand at a prep station. By the time I graduated high school, I figured I already knew everything they'd teach me so why waste the time and money?" Sliding a bite of tuna through the sauce, he added, "I also had a restaurant to run, though the guy Mom hired to keep the place going after Dad died tried to keep me out."

"That's shitty. What was his problem?"

"He thought I was an inexperienced kid who would run the place into the ground. Turns out he was right." Changing the subject, Nick said, "Did you go back to that mentor after graduation?"

She shook her head. "He promised me a guaranteed position but ended up selling the place and retiring to the South of France while I was still in school. The new chef felt no obligation to honor a promise he never made."

Now that was shitty. "He should have at least given you a chance."

Visibly shutting down, she examined her wineglass. "I had a reputation among the rest of the crew who were still there." Meeting his gaze, she shook her head. "Not a positive one."

Nick wanted to know more but could tell she wasn't interested in elaborating. Seeking a new, more positive topic, he asked, "How are things going with the staff? Is everyone on board now?"

Lauren swallowed the bite she'd taken before answering. "Yes, and I still owe you for that. If we hadn't gone up to the adventure park, I doubt I'd even have a staff right now. They've worked their tails off the last two days. We're still tweaking the dishes, but I've got food deliveries coming later in the week so we'll be ready with fresh food and a solid menu when the doors open."

"I've seen fliers posted around the island, and the locals are already talking about trying it out."

She stopped chewing. "They are?"

Nick didn't know why she was surprised. "Of course, they are. The Marina was dated but still popular before the remodel, and Will and Randy are practically royalty on the island so anything they touch gets plenty of support. Plus, they've heard about you and what you plan to offer."

"What have they heard?"

"That you're a fancy big city chef." He stabbed a Brussels sprout with his fork. "And that your food is amazing."

She nearly choked on her tuna. "How would they hear that? I haven't even served anything yet."

"You said you've been tasting dishes with the staff." Nick cut his last piece of tuna. "They must be talking and word travels fast in this little village."

Lauren didn't need to know that Nick had been doing some talking of his own, dropping a hint here and there about her skills. Now that he'd had a full meal, he was relieved to find his preliminary reviews had been accurate.

"I was already nervous about all the press Will has lined up." She dropped the fork and knife onto her plate and reached for her wine again. "Now I have the locals expectations to live up to? Yeah. No pressure."

As she emptied her glass, Nick rose from his chair and took the glass from her hand. "You're going to be fine."

"I'm going to stress the hell out is what I'm going to do."

Taking her hands, he pulled her to her feet. "Then it'll be my job to get you unstressed."

Skepticism showed in her eyes when she said, "How are you going to do that?"

Nick reached for the front of her shirt. "One button at a time."

————

NICK STAMATIS WAS VERY good at relieving stress. By the time he'd carried her to the bedroom—which was a first for her—Lauren could barely remember her own name let alone think about the restaurant. As promised, he'd taken his time, despite her nearly begging for him to hurry. He'd ignored her pleas, preferring instead to explore her body as if she were some uncharted territory that he'd recently discovered. By the time he'd touched, teased, and tasted every inch of her, Lauren's mind had turned to mush.

"Feeling better?" he asked as she lay sprawled across his chest.

As if all of her moaning and purring and the two times she'd screamed his name hadn't given him a clue.

"Much better." She turned her head to see his face. "You were *very* thorough."

"You're welcome." Nick played with a lock of her hair. "I like you, Riley."

She certainly hoped so considering their current circumstances. "Thanks. You're growing on me too."

"Do you ever see yourself having children?"

Not the question she expected. Lauren rolled into a sitting position and pulled the sheet up to cover her breasts. "Where the hell did that come from? I thought you didn't do relationships."

They were in this bed for that very reason. Because neither of them *did relationships*. Which sounded like a contradiction, but the sex came with an understanding. That's all it was. Just sex. If he'd changed his mind…

"I'm not asking you to have my babies," Nick said, but the expression on his face didn't match the words coming out of his mouth. The expression said *this matters*. That this was more than two adults enjoying each other. "Seriously," he said, pulling her back to him. "It was just a question. Looking at those old family pictures brought back memories and I just wondered what it must be like to have kids now. The world is so different from when we were young."

Lauren wasn't exactly an old woman. "What do you mean when *we* were young? I'm only thirty-one. It's not like video games and the internet were invented in the last few years."

Nick lifted an arm to rest above his head and she was temporarily distracted by how hot he was.

"Well, I'm thirty-six and I remember when kids actually played outside. And read books made of paper."

"Then you're ancient," she said, and earned a gentle bite on the shoulder. "To answer your question, no, I don't. I pretty much raised my brother. That was enough for me."

Dark eyes widened. "Really? You don't want kids?"

She didn't say that. He asked if she ever imagined herself having children. She would not repeat her mother's mistakes and have a kid without a husband. A husband meant marriage. Marriage required trust. Lauren would have to find someone who wouldn't cut and run when things got tough, or worse, play the nice guy role until the deal was done, and then start using his fists every time something didn't go his way.

Growing up around violence left a mark on your soul that never went away. She wouldn't do that to herself, or to an innocent child. But growing up poor wasn't a walk in the park either and she had no doubt if left to raise a child on her own, she'd fall right back into the cycle that had plagued her own childhood.

Even if she found a Mr. Mom who didn't mind bearing the brunt of child-rearing while she worked the hours being a chef required, Lauren would have to trust that he'd stick around for the duration. In her experience, men didn't do that.

Keeping the truth to herself, she said, "I take it you do?"

Nick went quiet as his eyes settled on something behind her. Finally, he said, "I don't know. I didn't plan on it."

One ambitious bout of sex with her could not have changed his mind on something so important.

"Are you having a midlife crisis?" she asked.

His eyes caught hers. "What?"

"Well..." She glanced up, doing a quick calculation. "If you live to be seventy-two, then you're in the middle right now."

A smile of pure joy split his face. "I *could* live to be seventy-two. Or maybe eighty-two."

"Why not go for ninety-two?" she said with a laugh.

With one swift move, he flipped her onto her back and hovered above her. "I think I will. But right now, what do you say we go for two?"

Panic tightened her gut. "Kids?" Lauren squeaked.

Nick's bark of laughter filled the room. "I meant sex," he mumbled, nuzzling into her shoulder. "You're something else, Riley."

She would have offered a witty comeback, but his lips were quickly sliding down below the sheet. "I'm... I... Ooh..."

Seconds later, kids were the furthest thing from her mind.

14

LAUREN FOUGHT OFF EXHAUSTION AS SHE PARKED HER CAR in front of a small building with a bright-pink awning over the door and the words SWEET OPAL'S BAKERY & CONFECTIONS emblazoned across the front window. This was apparently the site of some Tuesday ritual where Roxie and the other ladies, whom Lauren had started referring to as the gang, gathered to gab, gossip, and unwind with their favorite treats.

At least that's how Roxie had described the evening while insisting that Lauren should join them. Pilar's opened in less than a week and she'd have preferred to be in the kitchen, perfecting every dish down to the garnish, but Jackson had assured her that they could carry on for one evening without her. The others had tried to hide their relief when she'd slipped off her chef's jacket to go, but Lauren didn't hold it against them. No one had voiced a single complaint since the adventure park trip, and she'd been pushing them hard over the last few days.

She hadn't seen Nick since he'd left her place Monday morning. She'd expected him to leave some time during the night, but he'd stayed until she'd risen to go to work. Lauren wasn't sure how she felt about that. At least he hadn't brought up the kids thing again.

"We're over here," called Roxie from a table at the end of the patio. Will and Beth were already there, along with two little girls Lauren hadn't seen before. "Have a seat." Roxie tapped the white metal chair beside her.

A huge umbrella blocked the sun and shifted every time the little girl with the curly hair pushed at the table. She looked to be testing how much the thing could withstand.

"That's enough, Mary Ann," Beth said. "You promised me you'd behave."

"But I'm bored. I want my cupcake."

"You have to wait until the others arrive." To Will, she said, "I shouldn't have left the house so early."

"I'll take her in to see if Opal has any specials today." Will stood and offered her hand to the little girl, who took it and then skipped across the patio without a care in the world.

To Lauren's surprise, the other little girl, the smaller of the two, shuffled around Roxie's chair and said, "Up." Two chubby arms hovered in the air, waiting for the order to be followed.

Lauren looked at the other two women. "Does she

want me to pick her up?"

"You don't have to," Beth said. "Daphne, honey, come sit with Mommy."

The cherub didn't budge. "Up," she said again.

Roxie lifted the little one onto her lap, but she slid right off and made her demand one more time to Lauren. Admiring the child's grit, she gave in. Once on the target lap, she stuck a thumb in her mouth and leaned back against Lauren's chest as if this was an everyday thing.

"I'm sorry," Beth said. "She never meets a stranger, as you can tell."

"I don't mind." And oddly, she didn't. Daphne's wavy brown hair smelled like strawberries, while her chubby cheeks puffed in and out as she sucked on the tiny digit. Lauren pictured having a little girl of her own. Would she have blond hair, like hers, or maybe dark like Nick's?

Stunned by the unwelcome conjecture, she silently scoured the thought from her brain.

"Did you hear that, Lauren?"

She looked up to find the women looking her way. "I'm sorry. What?"

"I asked how the restaurant is coming along?" Beth repeated.

"Oh. Good. We've locked in the menu but now we're tweaking the dishes to make them as flavorful as possible. The waitstaff is also learning the menu so they'll be ready when the doors open."

As soon as the last word was out, Lauren found herself staring at the face of another munchkin. This one a little boy with dark hair and a very handsome face. "I'm Conner," he said. "Why you holding Daphne?"

"Because she told me to," she answered. "Nice to meet you, Conner."

"He's mine," Callie said, taking the chair beside Will's empty one. "That's Lauren, baby. She's new to the island."

"Where you from?" the inquisitive one asked.

"I grew up in Boston. Where are you from?"

The boy blushed. "Right here, silly." Turning, he spotted another little girl coming their way. "Oh, no," Lauren heard him say. "Not Pilar."

So this was the unofficial namesake of her restaurant.

"Who are you?" the new arrival demanded as she stopped beside the boy. "Why you holding my cousin?"

Lauren was starting the think the universe was messing with her. Why else would she suddenly find herself the center of every child's attention?

"Manners," Sid said to her daughter. "What have I told you about how to talk to adults?"

"You said to be nice. I am being nice," the girl defended. "She's got Daphne."

"She isn't stealing her." Sid took a seat next to Lauren. "I don't know where she gets this bossy attitude."

Beth burst out laughing. "It's a total mystery."

"Nobody yanked your chain, curly."

Lauren doubted she would ever get used to the dynamics in this group.

"Is everyone here?" Will said upon returning with Mary Ann.

"Henri is missing," Callie replied. "She said she had to make a stop on the way."

"Here she comes," Roxie said, nodding toward the parking lot.

The woman in question exited a blue Volkswagen Beetle and Mia climbed from the passenger seat. Lauren heard Roxie say, "About time," under her breath.

Before she could ask what that meant, the women joined the group and Will disappeared back inside only to return seconds later with a plump older woman draped in a ruffled pink apron. Her bright-blue eyes went right to Lauren.

"We have a newcomer, I see."

"This is Lauren Riley," Sid said. "She's the new chef over at Pilar's."

"That's my restant," cut in the little one with the same name.

"I heard," Opal replied. "Nice to meet you, Lauren, and welcome to Anchor Island. We're happy to have you."

"Thanks. I'm happy to be here." She hadn't been able to say those words and sincerely mean them in a long time. If ever.

"Does everyone know what they want?"

Lauren glanced around for a menu. "Do I need to go inside to see the options?" she asked.

"Oh, you need a menu." Opal whipped a small laminated sheet from the pocket of her apron. "The rest of these ladies are regulars so I guess they forgot you haven't been here before."

"Prepare yourself," Sid said. "Opal makes the best desserts you'll ever have in your life."

She'd sampled dishes from some of the best pastry chefs on the East Coast so Lauren doubted that could be true. Still, a sweet was a sweet and she had a deep abiding love for anything chocolate. Which is what drew her to an obvious choice.

"Is the chocolate heaven cup as good as it sounds?" she asked.

"Better," Sid assured her.

"Then that's what I'll have."

The rest of the group placed their orders, and then Sid and Will took the kids to see a dog at the other end of the patio in order to keep them entertained until the treats arrived. Lauren caught Henri whisper something to Mia, who looked as if she wanted to be anywhere else. The next thing Lauren knew, Mia had moved to Sid's empty seat beside her.

"You must be excited for the opening," she said.

Excited, panicked, and totally freaked the hell out were more like it. "I am. We're just about ready, but I almost wish I'd done a soft launch."

Mia cut a quick glance to Henri and then looked away. What exactly was up with these two?

"A soft launch?" she said, only half listening.

"It's when a restaurant opens without a lot of fanfare in order to test things first. Then a large scale opening happens once they work out the kinks."

"We could still do that," Will said, interrupting their conversation.

Lauren hadn't seen her return to the table. "We could do what?"

"Have a trial run." Will waved a hand to indicate the group around the table. "If everyone here brings their significant others, we could have a pre-launch meal to help you test the food and staff."

"I bet Tom and Patty would come, too," Beth offered.

These were not names Lauren knew.

"If we can get a babysitter for the twins, Sam and I will come," Callie said.

They were only four days away from opening. How were they going to get a pre-launch dinner in and still have time to adjust for any issues?

"I'm not sure we'll have time. We'd need a period after to address any necessary changes."

Will lifted Pilar onto her lap. "What about tomorrow?"

"You've got the meeting with the Ferrero family tomorrow night," Roxie reminded her.

"Crap. How about Thursday?" She looked to be asking Roxie, who smiled.

"You're free Thursday night."

"Can we bring the kids?" Beth asked. "If Tom and Patty come, then that would eliminate our babysitters, but I wouldn't want them to miss it either."

This was moving way too fast.

"There's a kid's menu," Roxie said. "If you're going to test the food, you might as well test all of it."

Lauren couldn't believe these women were willing to drop everything on such short notice just to help her out. Could they really do this? The staff was ready, and the dishes had almost been perfected. Front of house had started training yesterday morning and since most had worked at the Marina, they'd picked things up quickly. All she needed were the fresh ingredients, and Wyatt would likely help her out with the fish if she showed up at the pier at dawn.

"Are you all sure about this?"

"We're talking about after five, right?" Callie said.

An evening service would give the most time to prep.

"Sure. How about six thirty?" Lauren asked.

There were nods all around as cell phones were pulled from purses and pockets to text spouses. Fifteen minutes later, all had confirmed while, as Sid had promised, Lauren enjoyed the most decadent chocolate cupcake she'd ever tasted in her life. Not until an hour later on her drive home did the reality set in. Pilar's would seat a party of fourteen plus four kids in less than forty-eight hours for a full menu tasting.

She could only pray the staff didn't kill her when she told them the news.

————

NICK ASSURED himself that he was only checking in with a friend. The fact that during the check-in he could find out what was happening at Pilar's was a minor coincidence. He hadn't heard from Lauren since Monday morning when he'd made the short walk back to his place. Granted, that was only thirty-six hours ago, and they'd made no plans for when they would talk or meet up next. Why would they? She was busy trying to open a restaurant.

And Nick was busy imagining all the things that could be going wrong that he could help fix. A fact Lauren would likely resent.

Her ambition and independent spirit were two of the traits he liked most about her. There was also her complete lack of pretense as well as the unexpected displays of vulnerability. Nick had glimpsed the woman behind the wall. The woman with nerves of steel and a heart full of scars. She could talk a mean game, cook like a master, and bring a man to his knees. All of which she'd done on Sunday evening.

The simple fact that he hadn't been able to get her out of his head ever since should have sent him running, but Nick was tired of running.

"Hey, man," Jackson said as he joined Nick at the end of the bar. "How's it going?"

"That's what I was going to ask you." The crowd at O'Hagan's Pub was quiet on a Tuesday evening, which was why Nick had picked this location. "Four days and counting?"

"It's been tough but things are coming along."

"Tough?" Lauren had made it sound as if things were easily falling into place.

"She's hard to please, man." The bartender approached and Jackson ordered a beer. "We must have made some of these dishes fifty times now, and she finds something wrong with all of them. I don't know what she wants. Hell, none of us do."

Nick understood the situation from both sides. No chef sent food out of the kitchen that didn't meet their standards, but the staff couldn't read her mind either. And there was a good chance the food she was rejecting would more than meet the customers' expectations.

"I thought things got better after the adventure park."

"You know about that?"

Well aware of his friend's fear of heights, he leaned away and confessed, "That was my idea."

Jackson spun on his stool. "You're the reason I hauled my ass up a hill blindfolded?"

"It worked, didn't it?"

"That's cold, buddy. I'll remember this."

"Forget about the park. What about now? Is anyone thinking about walking?"

"No. She's actually pretty cool to work for. Calm. Patient. We just don't know how to get what she's wanting." The bartender returned with his drink, and he said, "Thanks, Cal," before continuing. "When she tests the individual components, there's no problem. But then we put them together and she either doesn't like the flavor combination or the balance is off. The menus are printed and ready, but she keeps talking about making changes. If we have to start over, there's no way we'll be ready by Saturday."

The woman was her own worst enemy.

"Maybe this is nerves. As the time gets closer, she'll calm down and run with what you've done so far."

"I don't know, man." He shook his head while lifting his beer. "She gets more anxious every day. This morning she started talking so fast that none of us understood a word she said."

Just as she'd been on Sunday when she'd greeted Nick like a human tornado. This time, he couldn't talk her down without revealing this visit with Jackson, and though his intentions were in the right place, Nick doubted she'd appreciate his efforts.

"Keep trying is all I can say. She's bound to relax eventually."

"That's what we're hoping." The older man leaned his elbows on the bar. "After she pulled my scared black ass up that death hill, I'm willing to follow her into the fire. I just hope she doesn't get us all scorched."

That made two of them.

15

LAUREN HAD NO IDEA HOW LONG SHE'D BEEN SITTING ON his front porch, or even how exactly she'd gotten there. All she knew was that on her way home from the bakery, she'd started to panic. Once she'd parked in front of her cottage, her brain had told her to go find Nick. So she did. Except Nick wasn't home.

Growing cold, she lifted off the top step, ready to give up, when headlights appeared before her, forcing her to cover her eyes to block the glare.

"Lauren?" Nick said, bounding from the truck. "Are you okay?"

"I just stopped by," she said, suddenly feeling like an idiot. "You're probably tired. I should go."

Before she took two steps, he cut her off. "What's wrong?"

Heart racing, she shook her head. "I shouldn't bother you."

This wasn't like her. When the anxiety hit, she dealt with it on her own. Men didn't like messy, and if she wanted to keep whatever casual thing they had going, then Lauren needed to keep her mess out of sight.

"You aren't bothering me. Come inside."

She *really* wanted to do that. Conflicted, she crossed her arms, uncrossed them, then crossed them again. "Are you sure? I know it's late…"

Nick pried her arms loose and took her by the hand. "I'm sure." Tugging her toward the cottage, he added, "Let me help."

How could he know those were the words she needed to hear?

Clinging to his hand, she followed him inside and Nick pulled her to the couch. "Sit down while I'll get you some water."

Lauren would have preferred whiskey, but alcohol would only make this worse. Her efforts to drink the demons away had always ended badly. While he fetched the water, she focused on her breathing. One breath at a time. In and out. Deep breath. Hold. Exhale.

"Here you go." He put the glass in her hand and then sat down beside her. "Take your time."

The man was a freaking saint. All the more reason she shouldn't be here.

"It's nothing, really," she said. "I'm fine." Her voice hitched and she took another deep breath.

"Why don't we go out back? The moon should be

bright on the water and we can sit and listen to the waves. That always makes me feel better."

Sitting quietly in the dark sounded like a good idea so she nodded her agreement and followed him to the sliding glass door.

Once outside, he led her to the Adirondack chairs, then said, "Have a seat and I'll be right back."

Lauren didn't want to be alone, but he was gone before she could stop him. Holding her drink with both hands, she perched on the edge of the chair and focused on the waves crashing in the distance. The moon was bright and glared off the water as if it were a shifting mirror. The rhythm of the ebb and flow matched her breathing and she felt herself begin to relax.

"Sit back," Nick said, returning with a blanket. She did as ordered and he draped the heavy material across her lap, then tucked it in along her sides. "Good?"

The simple gesture nearly made her cry. Speechless, she nodded, and he settled into the chair beside hers. They stayed that way, in silence for several minutes. As time passed and the ocean continued to roll in and back out, Lauren's lungs expanded and her heartbeat eased back to normal levels.

"Thank you," she finally said.

"For what?" he asked.

Lauren looked his way. "For being so nice to me. I know I'm not easy to deal with sometimes."

Nick leaned his head back against the chair.

"Everyone has their quirks. That's what Nota says anyway."

"Nota sounds like a wise woman."

"There has to be some benefit that comes from eight plus decades on this planet. Do you want to tell me what happened?"

This was the reason she was here. Lauren knew that now.

"I went to a girls' night thing with Roxie tonight. When I made an off-the-cuff comment that I wished I could try the food on a few customers before we opened the doors, they all volunteered."

"Volunteered?" he repeated.

"Yeah. I agreed to serve fourteen adults and four kids a full tasting menu on Thursday night."

Saying the words aloud brought the anxiety back.

"That's good. You can get some feedback before Saturday and have a day in between to make any changes."

If only it was that easy. "There's one problem."

"What? Is the staff not ready?"

She sighed and closed her eyes. "I'm not ready."

A warm hand wrapped around hers. "Lauren, if you aren't ready in two days, you aren't going to be ready in four."

"What if I'm never ready?"

Nick kissed the back of her hand. "You're an amazing chef, and you've put together a talented team. Now all you have to do is share your food. That's it. We don't save peoples' lives or right the wrongs of the world. We feed people. So do that, Lauren. Feed people."

"You make it sound so easy."

"It can be."

He had a point. "What was it you promised the other night? To unstress me?"

Nick glanced up to the stars. "I did."

"Then now would be a good time to do that."

His deep laughter made her smile. "I thought I just did."

Lauren tossed off the blanket and rose to her feet. "Not as thoroughly as you did on Sunday." After setting her glass in the sand, she lowered onto his lap. "I'm still feeling a bit tense in places."

A dark brow arched high. "Really? I should do something about that then."

Leaning in for a kiss, she said, "Yes. Yes, you should."

―――――

NICK COULD GET USED to this. A thought that scared the shit out of him. He'd never been the cuddle-after-sex type, but that's exactly what he was doing. And doing it willingly. If Lauren knew what he was thinking, he might never see her again.

The purpose for taking their conversation to the bedroom had been for Nick to help relieve her stress, but the treatment had gone both ways. If Lauren practically purring in his arms was any indication, she'd forgotten—at least temporarily—about her earlier fears. But Nick was feeling pretty relaxed himself. And content. Something he couldn't recall ever experiencing before. At least not since his father died.

Between the revelations Nota had shared and his growing feelings for Lauren, Nick found himself picturing a real future, with all the possibilities he'd never allowed himself to dream of. A development he needed to keep to himself for now.

"What did you do after your restaurant closed?" Lauren asked.

He considered giving a vague answer, but was truthful instead. "I didn't know what to call it at the time, but now I know that I grieved the loss the same way that I grieved for Dad. Only losing his business brought an added layer of guilt." Nick twirled a lock of her hair between his fingers. "I drank. A lot. Mia would say I became unbearable, and she'd be right."

"But you're still cooking so you didn't give up," Lauren pointed out.

"By then there wasn't much else I *could* do. I had one marketable skill and once I crawled out of my own pity party, I went back to the kitchen." Working for someone else had been an eye-opening experience, and he'd wanted to quit every day for the first year. Eventually, he stopped looking back and began moving forward. "I worked my way up until I finally landed an executive chef position in Atlantic City."

Lauren leaned up on her elbow. "*You* were an executive chef?"

She didn't have to sound so surprised. "I was. Three kitchens and fifty or so staff. I oversaw the daily operations for all of them, and I don't think I slept for three years."

"That sounds like a dream."

Did she miss the no sleep part?

"You're nuts if you think that sounds like a dream. I lost twenty pounds, my hair thinned, and I had zero social life." He pulled her back into the crook of his arm. "When Mia came to me about moving down here to take care of Nota—already armed with the offer to run Dempsey's kitchen—I couldn't pack fast enough."

"You left all of that for here?" she whispered.

"I left all of that for Nota," Nick corrected. "The island took some getting used to, but once you take a few deep breaths and realize life *can* move at a normal pace, you adjust."

"I don't know that I'll ever get used to it." She leaned closer and slid a leg over his. "My whole life has been a constant hustle. Roxie told me I need to relax, but how do you do that?"

To this he had an answer. "When I first got here, I had the same thought. People would be headed somewhere, and then stop to talk to every person they passed as if they had all the time in the world. But you know what I figured out?"

"What?"

"They do."

She looked up at him. "They do what?"

"Have all the time in the world."

"No one has all the time in the world," she argued.

"They do if they have their priorities straight."

Lauren was not giving up. "If something is a priority, then you bust your ass to get it done. Acting like you have nothing to do is the complete opposite of that."

"Taking your time doesn't mean acting like you have nothing to do. It means knowing that the world is not going to stop spinning because you take an hour to do something comfortably instead of killing yourself to get it done in half the time." She opened her mouth to argue, and Nick cut her off. "Take cooking for example. You can wish a pork loin would cook in five minutes, but that doesn't change how long it actually takes. And if you try to rush it, you end up with a dish you can't serve, making all of that effort for nothing."

When she didn't immediately respond, he thought he'd won the point. He should have known better.

"If you want something to cook faster, you turn up the heat. Everyone knows that."

He couldn't help but laugh. "Have I told you how adorably annoying you are?"

That earned him a poke in the ribs. "I am *not* annoying."

"Yes, you are." Nick kissed the top of her head. "So how about you? Where did you pay your dues?"

Lauren tensed against him. "Lots of places."

Considering she was thirty-one and went to culinary school, she'd only been working for eight to ten years depending on when she went in. Even adding the experience gained before going to school, he couldn't imagine the word *lots* applied.

"How many are we talking about? Three? Four?" Her response was mumbled and Nick failed to make out the words. "I didn't catch that."

"Nine," she said louder.

That couldn't be true. "No way. I'm five years older than you and I've only worked at six."

Rolling onto her back, she tucked the sheet beneath her elbows and crossed her arms, her eyes locked on the ceiling. "I started when I was seventeen and went through three jobs before going to school right after I turned twenty. I graduated at twenty-three," she continued in a flat tone. "Then I worked at six different places in the last seven and a half years."

Nick had never known anyone who changed jobs that often. Knowing there had to be a reason, he turned to face her and asked, "Why so many?"

Jaw tight and lips pinched into a line, she continued to stare at the ceiling. Every thought crossed her face and he could see that she didn't want to answer.

"Lauren." With a slow blink, she met his gaze. "Why so many?"

Returning her focus to the ceiling fan, she sighed. "I'm sure you'll find this shocking, but I'm not a people person."

Most chefs weren't. That's why they chose the kitchen instead of being out on the floor.

"Anyone who picks this profession could say the same."

She bit the inside of her cheek. "Nick, people don't like me."

"I like you."

"You like having sex with me. Not the same thing."

Turning her to face him, he said, "I like being with you. Period. Sleeping with you is a bonus."

Her blue eyes went wide. "That sounds dangerously close to a relationship. We don't do relationships, remember?"

Taking a risk, Nick trailed a thumb along her cheek. "What if that's changed?"

Body stiff, she looked away. "I don't know how to answer that."

Relieved that she hadn't run for the exit, he said, "Take your time." Leaning forward, he kissed her pursed lips. "I'm willing to wait."

LAUREN LAY AWAKE LONG after Nick had drifted off to sleep.

I'm willing to wait.

What was she supposed to do with a statement like that? Lauren wasn't deaf to the gossip. Nick had a reputation for being a playboy, and he'd apparently been loud and proud about his policy to never settle down. Though most women would find that a character flaw, she'd seen it as an insurance policy that he'd never expect more from her.

Now the jerk had gone and changed the game?

Exactly *what* was he willing to wait for? For Lauren to suddenly become someone she wasn't? For her to ignore everything she knew about men and relationships and how they were both a losing proposition? Having a front row seat to her mother's string of bad breakups—which often came with black eyes and always an empty bank account—had taught Lauren to never let anyone have control of her life.

Glancing to her left, she tried to picture Nick as any of the men her mother had dated. One by one, she ticked off the common traits. Selfish. Lazy. Possessive. Irresponsible. The man beside her was none of those things. If anything, he'd proved to be the opposite in every way. He'd shared his knowledge while giving her a place to vent and a shoulder to lean on. He'd seen her at her worst and never flinched. If anything, Nick was too good for Lauren, not the other way around.

No. This was all an illusion. They'd only known each other for a few weeks. Given time, history *would* repeat. He'd get tired of her neurosis and find someone else. Or she'd work too much and he'd get bored. No matter the reason, they'd end up hating each other and then be stuck on this puny island, unable to avoid crossing paths.

At least if she drew the line now, they might be able to stay friends.

Decision made, Lauren slid from the bed as slowly as she could and gathered her clothes that had been scattered around the room before tip-toeing out of the room. Minutes later, she slipped out the front door, careful not to make a sound. The light of the moon guided her home, and as she crawled into her own bed, she expected to feel relief. As if she'd caught herself before doing something incredibly stupid.

But relief didn't come. And neither did sleep. Because the truth was, she'd already done the stupidest thing of all.

She'd fallen in love with Nick Stamatis.

16

"WHERE ARE THE PLATES?" LAUREN YELLED.

"In the warmer, Chef," Jackson replied.

"Who put them in there?" she demanded, her hands on her hips.

"You did, Chef."

Lauren took a deep breath. Now was not the time to start tormenting her staff. When she'd broken the news about the pre-launch dinner the previous morning, no one had batted an eye. A reminder that she had a seasoned team used to serving far more than a dozen plus a few kids. They'd worked throughout the day perfecting each dish and continued prepping through early evening, after which Lauren had locked the doors, feeling good about their progress.

She'd received one text from Nick, which she'd ignored, and then she'd spent the evening praying he wouldn't show up at her door. When he didn't, she brushed off the disappointment, reminding herself that this was for the best. Nick clearly wanted something Lauren did not. He couldn't blame her when the rules had been clear from the beginning.

Besides, the restaurant needed all of her attention right now.

There had been a slight hiccup first thing this morning when Will had called to increase the number for the dinner from fourteen to sixteen adults. Thankfully, the number of children had remained the same. Axel had taken the message and not bothered to ask who the new additions would be. Lauren assumed Will had invited potential wedding clients so they could taste her food, since Pilar's would be doing the catering for most Destination Anchor events.

"Hello!" someone called from the dining room, and Lauren recognized her boss' voice. "Can we do anything to help?"

Stepping into the pass, Lauren greeted Will and Randy Navarro with a wave. She didn't think she'd ever get used to how big Randy was. At least six foot five, the man could easily be mistaken for a professional wrestler if it weren't for the ever-present smile on his handsome face. On more than one occasion she'd seen him at the fitness center, which he owned, of course, lifting upwards of three hundred pounds.

"Do you need us to move tables or anything?" Randy asked.

They'd brought in four members of the waitstaff for

the evening, and Lauren had worked with them to make the necessary table adjustments. "Already done." She called to the break room in the back, "Carla, our first guests have arrived."

Carla Fennell, a woman in her mid-fifties who had been the lead hostess at the Marina for more than ten years, shuffled into view. "I'm on it."

Lauren checked the clock on the wall. If the other diners arrived at the designated time, they had another ten minutes before the meal officially began. Because the point was to get feedback on the entire menu, they'd decided to send the dishes out family style starting with the appetizers. They wouldn't get to practice individual plating, but this night was about taste more than presentation.

The rest of the waitstaff headed for the dining room in their black pants, pressed turquoise shirts—the official color of Pilar's—and pristine new aprons. Only one was new and Lauren had faith that the more experienced servers would keep an eye on him. When she turned to survey the kitchen, Lauren couldn't suppress a smile. Jackson, Mona, Deborah, Dodge, Brit, Penny, and Axel were at their stations, fully focused and ready to go.

She had never been prouder or more nervous in her life.

For a split second, Lauren wished Nick was there to calm her nerves. A clear sign that putting distance between them was the right thing to do. She could hear her mother's voice in her head. *Never depend on anyone but yourself.* Words Lauren had lived by for as long as she could remember, and she'd done just fine so far.

But have you?

Shaking the disloyal thought away, Lauren took a final pass around the kitchen and heard more voices in the dining room. Curious, she peeked through the pass and watched as some of the children she'd met at Opal's were wrestled into high chairs. Since her previous encounters had been with the women in the group, none of the husbands looked familiar. Except for Roxie's boyfriend, Alex Fielding. And she'd seen the one sitting closest to Beth working out with Randy at the fitness center.

Will caught her attention. "Lauren, come out so I can introduce you to everyone."

The moment of truth had arrived. She turned, took a deep breath, and got a thumbs-up from Jackson.

"You've got this, Chef."

She appreciated the show of support. Shoulders back, Lauren made her way to the dining room and crossed to the gathered diners.

"Everyone, have a seat so I can introduce our star chef who is about to feed us what I'm sure will be an amazing meal."

Will waited for the crowd to settle and Lauren noticed three empty seats at the end of the table. She started to count those present, but the introductions began before she reached half a dozen.

"First we have Tom and Patsy Dempsey. They own Dempsey's Bar & Grill and are Joe and Lucas' parents."

Lauren's stomach dropped to her knees. Why hadn't anyone told her the owners of the most successful eatery on the island would be here?

"That's Gram and Poppy," Mary Ann corrected.

"Only to us," Pilar informed her.

The group laughed as the mothers instructed their offspring to hush.

"Beside them we have Joe and Beth and their daughters Mary Ann and Daphne, you know Roxie and Alex, then there's Sid and Lucas with Pilar."

"This is my restant," the child announced.

"Yes, it is, sweetie," Randy assured her.

"On this side we have Sam and Callie Edwards with their son Connor," Will continued, "and Henri, of course."

As she got to the empty chairs, the restaurant door swung open and Lauren looked over to see Mia walk through, followed by Nota and Nick. They must have been the two added to the group.

Her body stiffened as they approached and she struggled to keep her expression neutral. Nick smiled when their eyes met, and Lauren looked away.

"Thank you, all, for coming tonight," she said, not waiting for Will to introduce the newcomers. "We have a full tasting prepared so you'll get to try all of the options. Feedback is welcome and appreciated, good or bad, but we've done our best to make everything as tasty as possible so hopefully you'll be more than satisfied." Gesturing toward the waitstaff, she said, "Carla and her team will get your drink orders, and the appetizers will start coming out shortly. Thank you again, and I hope you enjoy the meal."

Without another word, she spun and marched toward the kitchen, encountering Nick and Nota on the way.

"Lauren," he said as she passed.

"Not now, Nick, I'm busy."

Gut churning, she swept through the kitchen door, stopping on the other side to catch her breath. Her heart had attempted to beat out of her chest the moment he'd looked at her, and she'd nearly embarrassed herself by running into his arms.

He couldn't possibly mean so much to her considering how little they knew each other. She'd been on the island for less than six weeks. No one fell in love that fast. This was nothing more than her being dropped into a new place with no connections and Nick being the one person with whom she shared something in common.

He was a chef. He understood what she was going through opening her first restaurant. So they'd slept together. So what. Lauren had done the no-strings sex plenty of times in the past and never crossed the line. She never let her heart get involved, and she would not be stupid enough to make that mistake now.

"Chef?" She looked up to find Jackson watching her with concern in his big brown eyes. "You okay?"

Lauren stepped away from the door and rolled up her sleeves. "I'm fine. Are we ready?"

"The oysters are plated and the glazed scallops will be up in four minutes."

Putting Nick out of her mind, she took her position at the pass. "All right, guys. Let's do this."

———

NICK DIDN'T NEED a sign to tell him that he'd screwed up. They'd had an arrangement with established boundaries that he'd stomped right over.

Lauren clearly hadn't known that he'd be there. He hadn't even known himself until two hours ago. Nota had apparently run into Will at the coffee shop and landed an invitation. Why she and Mia needed him to tag along he didn't know, but they'd insisted and here he was.

Lauren had every right to put the brakes on, and he didn't blame her for backing off. But he also didn't appreciate her giving him the silent treatment. If she wanted to end things entirely, the least she could do was have the guts to tell him so.

When he and Nota reached the table, Mia nearly jerked his arm out of the socket as she maneuvered him out of the way to avoid having to sit next to Henri. He'd been half tempted to yank her back and leave her no option, but one woman pissed at him was enough for now. Henri had given him a knowing look with a mixture of humor and disappointment in her eyes. Nick had no idea what, if anything, was going on between her and his sister, but he hoped Mia wasn't stringing the poor woman along.

Then the truth dawned. Mia dragged him here to run interference. Whether to keep Henri at a distance or to keep Nota in the dark was the question, but whatever the purpose, he didn't appreciate being used.

The appetizers arrived on large platters, one for each end of the table, and were served with about five minutes in between. He did his best to catch reactions from around the table and as far as Nick could tell, the food was a hit from the start. Personally, he'd have added more orange maple sauce to the wings and left the apple cider gastrique off the glazed scallops, but those were personal taste issues and not substantial criticisms.

The meal progressed with a collection of noodle dishes. Pilar's offered an interesting twist on shrimp and grits—unusual coming from a New England chef—and the crab mac & cheese was a favorite around the table. A clam dish plus two vegetarian options followed, and Nick noticed the servings getting smaller. Smart, considering they had yet to reach the entree round.

Empty plates were constantly being cleared as new dishes arrived. Once they'd reached the end of the appetizers, Lauren returned from the kitchen. She looked professional, capable, and determined *not* to look his way.

"I hope you're enjoying the meal so far," she said, and received murmured affirmations from around the table. "I wanted to tell you a little about our entrees, which are coming up next. We have Pilar's special catch of the day, which tonight is mahi tuna caught just this morning. We also have non-seafood items including grilled rosemary chicken, a pistachio crusted pork loin, and a New York strip steak. The steak will be served medium so a bit pink inside, but if you'd like it cooked a little more, let a server know and we can do that for you. There's no hurry so take your time finishing up what's already on the table and the entrees will be on their way soon."

Conversations resumed as Lauren went back to the kitchen. Nick lifted the napkin off his lap and left it on his chair as he slid away to catch her.

"Hey," he said seconds before she could disappear into the kitchen. "Talk to me for a second."

Lauren stopped, but she didn't look happy. "I've got a lot going on right now."

"I know you're busy. I just wanted to say…" What the hell did he want to say? He was sorry? He didn't mean what he'd said the other night? That was bullshit. He'd meant every word. "I just want to make sure you're okay."

"I'm a big girl, Nick. I'm fine."

He stepped back with his hands up. "You're right.

You've got this." Unable to resist, he added, "Everyone at the table says the food is great."

She shook her head, her jaw tight. "You can stop playing the mentor role now. I don't need the pep talks anymore. Or anything else."

With that parting shot, she returned to the kitchen, leaving Nick standing in the empty corner feeling like a fool. This was his own fault. He'd known the rules, and he'd broken them. Lauren had every right to call him on it.

Returning to his seat, he kept his head down and pretended he hadn't just had his ass handed to him.

"What was that?" Mia whispered.

"Leave it alone," he snapped.

"What are you two whispering about?" Nota said loud enough for everyone at their end of the table to hear.

Lifting his fork, Nick said, "Nothing, Nota."

"Are you seeing Lauren Riley?" Mia asked, making sure their grandmother didn't overhear this time.

"No."

"Then what was—"

"Do you want to talk about why you refused to sit in this seat?" he asked through gritted teeth. Mia leaned away, her lips tight. "I didn't think so."

They ignored each other for the rest of the meal, which went on for another hour. Nick wanted to leave as soon as the final dishes were cleared, but Nota was deep in conversation with Patty Dempsey, and Mia was showing off her island mural. Lauren returned to the table one last time to thank them all for coming and asked that if they had any comments could they please forward them to Will at the Destination Anchor offices.

He had no doubt the reviews would be positive. Pilar's would be an island staple in no time, and Lauren would be a star among the locals, hating every moment that the spotlight was on her and not her food. Despite what was going on between them, he was proud of her. She was right. Tonight she'd proved that she didn't need him.

The problem was that now he needed her.

17

"THAT'S THE LAST OF IT, CHEF," JACKSON SAID AS THE team finished the cleanup.

The dinner had been a success, leaving Lauren both optimistic and exhausted. Serving a full dining room would be more challenging in countless ways, but her staff came through tonight. When a member struggled to keep up, another stepped in to help. When the sauce for the pork loin broke, Dodge whipped up a new one in record time.

To think, she'd likely still be looking for good cooks if Nick hadn't intervened and opened her eyes.

Not that she wanted to think about Nick right now. Lauren had no idea how he'd gotten an invitation to the dinner. He probably thought she'd *need* him and used his grandmother as a way to weasel his way in. Heaven forbid she handle anything without him.

That she'd felt a rush of relief when he'd walked in

was beside the point. She didn't *want* to need him. She couldn't *let* herself need him.

"Are you coming with us?" Mona said, snapping Lauren from her thoughts.

"Coming where?"

"To O'Hagan's. This night calls for a celebration."

"What's O'Hagan's?" Lauren really should explore the island more.

"A little dive bar not far from here," she replied.

"Come with us," Deborah added. "The celebration won't be complete without the team captain."

Though tired, Lauren didn't feel like going home. Especially when Nick might show up unannounced. Avoiding him was childish and cowardly, but the truth was she didn't trust herself. He'd come too close to breaking through her defenses, and she needed time and distance to build them back up.

"I'm driving so I can't drink," she said.

"I'm the designated driver," Axel said.

"Me, too," Brit chimed in. "One of us will get you home and then pick you up tomorrow before work. Your car will be fine here overnight."

In that case, there wasn't any reason not to tie one on. "I guess I'm in."

Lauren couldn't remember the last time she'd gone drinking with coworkers. Or the last time she'd been invited. She'd always watched everyone pile out of the kitchen at the end of the night, headed for the closest bar, but no one had ever bothered to include her. They either hadn't thought to ask or hadn't noticed her absence.

Lauren climbed into Axel's VW Bus along with Dodge, Jackson, and three of the waiters. They arrived at O'Hagan's in a matter of minutes and once inside, she realized Mona had not been joking. The place was a dive bar in the best of ways. Dark, small, and full of character. The decor was mostly neon signs mixed with beach paraphernalia.

A surfboard leaned against a wall below a Budweiser light. A snorkel mask hung next to a giant bottle cap. The only other theme appeared to be pirates. Pictures of them dotted the walls.

"What's the thing with pirates around here?" she asked Deborah as they crossed to a large empty table in the corner.

"You don't know?"

If she knew, why would she ask?

"I have no idea."

"This area was a hangout for Blackbeard, and it's where he was finally killed. There's an entire museum dedicated to him on the island, and we have a huge pirate festival every summer." She pulled out a chair to sit and Lauren did the same. "He's like a cult hero around here."

She wouldn't call a man known for pillaging and plundering to be a hero, but to each their own.

"Heya, Dodge," said the young waitress who approached the table. "Haven't seen you in a while."

The young man's blush was evident even in the darkened barroom. "Hey, Stacy. I meant to call but I've been busy, what with the restaurant and all."

Something told Lauren that was a lie.

"Sure, buddy." Turning to the others, she said, "What are we having, folks?"

"We'll need to start some tabs," Mona said. "The boss here is on mine."

"I can pay for my own drinks," Lauren assured her.

"Not tonight you can't."

Four others spoke up about starting tabs, and then the orders were taken. Lauren considered sticking with beer, but if they were celebrating, she might as well get what she really wanted. When her order arrived, the mix of lime, rum, and fresh mint was perfectly sweet and tart and she knew she'd be having a few more mojitos before the night was over.

Two hours later, she'd had more than a few.

"You were awesome," she told Jackson for the third time. "I mean it. You kept us on track tonight." Each *t* was accompanied by spit as she was quickly losing control of her lips. "I might be a little drunk," she announced.

"You're a lot drunk," Mona informed her as Jackson scratched his belly and laughed. "And so are the rest of us."

"Except Axel and Brit," Penny corrected.

Lauren tried to focus on the designated drivers, but

they were a bit hazy. "Way to take one for the team, guys."

"Happy to do it, Chef," Axel replied.

"He doesn't drink," Penny informed her in a loud whisper. "Says it isn't good for you."

"Very sensible of him."

"Last round, y'all," Stacy said. "Down 'em while you've got 'em. The doors close in ten minutes."

Well, that was no fun. "We just got started."

"You're welcome to keep the party going," the waitress said, "but you'll have to take it elsewhere."

Turning to Mona, Lauren said, "Where else can we go?"

"Home," the woman answered. "We're already going to feel like shit tomorrow. It's time to sleep this off."

Without warning, Lauren was lifted from her chair and plopped onto her feet. Turning, she found Jackson staring at her with a wide grin.

"What was that for?"

"You couldn't get up."

"I didn't get the chance to try."

"You tried twice and landed on your butt both times."

She had no memory of doing any such thing. A sure sign that Mona was right. Lauren was going to feel like hell tomorrow.

The group stumbled outside together, Deborah, Mona, and Lauren arm-in-arm. The two ladies were singing a tune Lauren didn't know so she hummed along. They parted ways, all returning to the vehicles they had arrived in, and before she knew it, Axel was shaking her awake.

"Chef, I need to know which house is yours."

"Oh." She sat up and wiped drool from her chin. "My cottage is the fourth one on the right." Looking around, she asked, "How did you know where I live? And where are the others?"

"I've already dropped them off. Jackson told me you live over here on Tuttles Lane, but he didn't know which house."

She couldn't remember ever telling Jackson where her place was. Lauren rubbed her eyes and realized she couldn't feel her teeth. How many damn mojitos did she have?

"Here you go," Axel said, pulling the van to a stop. Without looking, she opened the passenger door and slid out. "You want me to wait until you get inside?" he asked.

Anchor Island didn't exactly have a high crime rate and Lauren wasn't so drunk that she couldn't find her own front door. "I'll be fine. You go on home."

Smacking her teeth together to wake them up—did teeth even go to sleep—Lauren struggled to drag her keys from her pocket. As Axel drove away, she used the light of her cell phone screen to locate the correct key and stuck it in the lock, but for some reason, it wouldn't fit. She flipped it over, but still nothing.

"What the hell?" she said aloud. Using the phone, she checked the key again. This was definitely the right one.

Pointing the screen at the doorknob, she bent to get a closer look and tried again. Jiggling the knob, she said, "Why won't you work, damn it?"

A second later, the door opened and a deep voice said, "Because this isn't your house."

Blinking, she straightened, squinting to make out the figure silhouetted against a light inside. "Then whose house is it?"

Nick flipped on the porch light. "Mine. How much did you drink?"

"How do you know I've been drinking?" she asked, slurring her words.

"Because you smell like rum soaked toothpaste and you don't know where your own house is." Stepping back, he said, "Come in and I'll make you some coffee."

Lauren was not walking through that door.

"I don't need coffee. And I don't need you taking care of me." Losing her balance, she caught herself on the doorframe. "I've been taking care of myself since I was nine years old, and I'll keep taking care of myself without anybody's help. Including yours."

Nick sighed. "You can barely stand up on your own. Let me get my shoes and I'll walk you home."

The man hadn't heard a word she said. When he disappeared inside, she turned and managed to get down the steps without landing on her face.

"How many times do I have to tell him? I'm an independent woman. I've fought off bullies, creeps, perverts, and handsy dishwashers twice my size. I can damn well walk my own ass a hundred yards down this street."

She made it to the edge of his drive when she heard, "You're going the wrong way."

Stopping, she squinted into the darkness. *Why didn't this stupid island have streetlights?*

Gravel crunched behind her as he approached, and her inebriated brain decided this was the time to end things. Like ripping off a Band-Aid, she'd rip Nick Stamatis out of her life once and for all.

———

"WHERE DO YOU GET OFF?" she said, spinning on him and nearly falling over. "You said no relationships. You said we were on the same page. Then you get me into bed and you make me feel things for you that I don't want to feel and now the page is different. It's a new page. I don't like this page."

Nick knew better than to have this conversation when she was drunk.

"Just come inside. You need to sober up."

"What I need is for you to stop being so nice to me. And hot. You're even sexy with your hair messed up like that." Lauren blinked up at him. "Stop looking like that."

The last was said loud enough to echo off the cottages around them and Nick checked the house on his left. Juanita Spencer worked the counter at the island post office and was a main source of village gossip. If he didn't get Lauren inside soon, they would be the top story for at least a week, and any credibility she had as a head chef would be gone.

"We can talk about this in the house," he whispered.

"I'm not going in there with you!" she shouted, adding a foot stomp to make it a true tantrum.

A light went on next door and Nick made a split-second decision. Reaching for her arm, he bent and tossed Lauren over his shoulder. She squealed as he booked it for the porch. Right before reaching the door, he heard Juanita come outside and yell, "Hello?"

Clicking the door shut, Nick set her down in the living room and took a second to catch his breath.

"What was *that?*" she squawked, filling the air with the smell of rum. "I told you I didn't want to come in here."

"I just saved your ass from being the lead story of tomorrow's island gossip. Do you want Pilar's opening to be overshadowed by how its chef was drunk and waking up her neighbors at two in the morning?"

Her mouth snapped shut. "I wouldn't have had a reason to yell if you'd let me go home."

"Again, you were going the wrong way." He waved a hand in front of her face. "Can you even see straight right now?" The motion threw her off-balance and she stepped to the side, arms out like a surfer. "That's what I thought."

Nick crossed to the kitchen and grabbed a coffee pod from the cabinet. Popping the top on the machine, he dropped it in, slid a mug under the nozzle and snapped it shut. Once the coffee was brewing, he snagged a bottle of water from the fridge and the pain pills from the cabinet.

"Here." He set both on the island counter. "You'll probably still feel like shit tomorrow but these should help."

"Why do you keep doing this?" she asked, ignoring his offering and remaining near the couch.

Leaning against the counter behind him, Nick crossed his arms. "Doing what?"

"Taking care of me." She had the nerve to look offended.

"It's called basic human decency," he answered, tired and more than a little cranky. "Why didn't you answer my message?"

She dropped her eyes to examine the top of a chair. "I was busy."

"Bullshit." When her face jerked up, she swayed again. "Sit down before you fall down."

"I didn't ask to come in here. If I'm bothering you so much, then why didn't you let me leave?"

"Because I care about you," he snapped. "Not that you make it easy. Just sit down and take the pills. Once you drink the coffee, I'll walk you home and you can go back to pretending there's nothing between us."

Bottom lip extended, she dropped into the chair. "You're the one who changed the rules. No relationships. That's what you said."

He'd never told her the real reason for that statement, but regardless, she was right. He'd changed the rules. Maybe the rules needed to be changed, but that was not something they would resolve in her current condition.

"We're not having this conversation while you're drunk." Nick put the coffee on the table in front of her, then opened the pill bottle and set it and the water beside the mug. "Do yourself a favor and take the medicine."

Lowering onto the couch, Nick ran his hands over his face with a sigh. This was not how he'd seen his night going, but at least Lauren had landed at his door instead of Juanita's. He watched her take the medicine, then sit back with the coffee mug cupped in her hands. Her eyes were fixed on something in the distance and it took several seconds for him to notice the silent tears.

Assuming the alcohol was the cause, he said, "Things will look better in the morning. Just drink the coffee."

"I don't like this feeling," she mumbled.

"Then you probably shouldn't drink again."

"I don't like needing you."

That was not what he expected. "Needing me?"

"I can't depend on you," she continued as if he hadn't spoken. "I can only depend on myself. That's what Mom taught me."

Understanding how easy it was to believe a false narrative, Nick said, "Your mom was wrong, Lauren.

Humans weren't made to go through life alone. You showed me that."

As if hearing his voice for the first time, she cut her gaze his way. "I did what?"

"After years of believing that love wasn't worth the risk, you walked into my life. And like all the times before, I thought something casual would be enough. That we'd have some fun and move on." He leaned forward, elbows on his knees. "But every time we're apart, all I can think about is when I'll see you again."

Another tear rolled down her cheek. "You'll walk away," she whispered. "Everyone walks away."

"Not everyone." Nick got up and offered a hand. "Come to bed, Lauren. If you want to leave in the morning, I won't ask you to stay. And if you don't want to see me again, I'll respect your wishes. But for now, just come to bed."

Eyes wide, she stared up at him. Every thought traveled across her face. Doubt. Fear. Longing.

"I just want to hold you," he assured her.

Lauren took his hand and set the mug on the table before rising to her feet. She followed him into the bedroom and slid in under the blankets as he held them up for her. Nick crawled in beside her and she curled against his side with her head on his shoulder. After kissing the top of her head, he pulled her tight against him.

If this was all she could give, then he'd take it.

18

THE POUNDING IN LAUREN'S HEAD DRAGGED HER OUT OF the darkness. Slowly easing her eyes open, she saw a blue glow coming from her left. She struggled to figure out where she was when something moved beside her. Sharp bristles brushed her shoulder as warm breath blew across her neck.

Her eyes snapped shut as snippets of memories flickered through her mind. With as little movement as possible, she patted her chest and then below her waist to find she was completely dressed. *Oh, thank goodness.* Breathing once more, she felt her stomach roll and pressed a hand against her mouth.

Desperate, she edged to the right and set one foot on the floor, then the other before letting her bottom slide off the mattress. Once free, she hopped up and tip-toed as fast as she could to reach the bathroom. Turning the knob, she shut the door as quietly as possible mere seconds before emptying her stomach into the toilet. Lauren couldn't remember the last time she'd vomited, and she had never tried to do so without making any noise.

Once the retching stopped, she sat down with her back to the cold tub and wiped her mouth with a handful of toilet paper. Taking slow, steady breaths, she listened for any movement on the other side of the door but heard nothing. Shoulders drooping with relief, she stayed on the floor until certain she could move without getting sick again.

Palms pressed to the cold tile, she tried to remember what led her to this point. There'd been the trip to O'Hagan's. Lots of mojitos. A couple baskets of nachos, which explained the taste of sour salsa in her mouth. Her next memory was Axel driving her home. He'd asked which house was hers and she'd told him. The fourth house on the right.

"Shit," she mumbled, leaning her head back on the side of the tub. The fourth house was Nick's. Hers was four beyond that.

She remembered arguing with Nick, though the details were faint. Then he'd carried her inside. The memory of being tossed over his shoulder made her nauseated and she deepened her breathing. Once the feeling passed, she tried to remember how they got to the bedroom. There were pain pills. A cup of coffee. And Nick asking her to come to bed.

She couldn't remember anything else. Pulling up her

knees, Lauren rested her forehead between them and closed her eyes. Concentrating, she saw Nick in the kitchen making coffee. Then he was on the couch, looking at her with sleepy brown eyes and saying, "...*all I can think about is when I'll see you again.*"

For so long Lauren had wanted to hear those words, yet they filled her with fear. The thought of leaving made her chest hurt, but staying would be the same as putting a loaded gun in Nick's hand. Leaving meant safety. Staying meant eventual heartbreak. Something she'd watched play out over and over and always with the same result.

Lifting herself off the floor, she locked her jaw and felt around for the sink. Turning the faucet on just enough to fill her hand, she rinsed out her mouth, then used her sleeve to dry off. Easing the door open, Lauren crept around the bed. The digital clock—the source of the blue glow—told her it was nearly four. Stopping at the door, she took one more look at the man who had become far too important in her life.

For a brief moment, she considered returning to the bed, but her mother's voice filled her ears again.

Men will hurt you every time, baby. Don't give 'em the chance.

The scene went blurry as tears filled her eyes, and Lauren walked away. Between the bedroom and the door she found her shoes, but she didn't put them on until she reached the porch. An owl's cry echoed in the distance as she made the short walk, and Lauren wondered if there might be another cottage available in the village. Saying she wanted to be closer to the restaurant would be a plausible excuse for the move. Not that she could put much distance between herself and Nick on such a small island, but any amount would be better than where she was now.

Once home, she locked the door, pressed her back against it, and slid to the floor. Sobs rocked her body and she let the tears fall. There was no reason to hold back now. No need to be quiet or hide the pain. In the morning, she would start over. She would rebuild the walls that Nick had so easily broken through.

Tonight, she just wanted to cry.

———

TEN DAYS and he'd kept his promise. Lauren's absence that next morning, followed by total silence after, sent the message loud and clear.

She was done.

Nick made no attempts to see or message her, and other than the few times he'd been outside when she'd passed by his house, their paths hadn't crossed. After the first few days, he'd come up with a theory just to save his own sanity and to keep him from doing anything stupid. The whole thing had been a matter of circumstance and bad timing.

Lauren walked into his life at a moment when Nick had gone from fearing death to envisioning a long future and all the possibilities that entailed. Like a dying man searching for water, she'd been his oasis. An illusion that could never be real. Lucky for them both, she'd suffered no such illusions.

"There you are." The voice startled Nick from his thoughts. "Why aren't you answering your phone?"

To avoid temptation, he'd begun leaving his phone in another room whenever possible. Today he'd come outside without it.

"I didn't want to be bothered," he lied. "What's going on?"

Mia shrugged and sat down beside him. "Nothing specific. I just wanted to check on you."

Who was the older sibling again? "Check on me?"

She stared out over the ocean. "Mostly. I know something was going on between you and Lauren Riley, and whatever it was didn't end well." Blocking the sun with her hand, she turned his way. "Are you okay?"

Kicking a bit of sand with his shoe, he said, "You know me. I never get serious."

"You were this time," Mia countered. "I saw it the night of the dinner. The look on your face when you came back to the table said things had gotten really serious."

"Only for one of us," Nick replied. Changing the subject, he said, "Did you know about these uncles we have? The ones in their seventies and eighties?"

Her gaze returned to the water. "Not until Grandma

and I went through the pictures for the photo albums. Why?"

"I was surprised. This is family we knew nothing about."

Mia sat up in her chair. "That's why you got serious with Lauren. Because you finally realized you aren't going to die young."

His sister was too damn quick. "I could still get hit by a bus tomorrow, but yes, I'm considering new possibilities."

"There aren't any buses on Anchor Island," she reminded him. "Now I wish I'd made those photo albums years ago."

In a moment of raw honesty, he said, "I wish you had, too."

Not that there was anyone in his past that he'd consider the one that got away. Unless he counted the recent past.

"So what happened?" she asked.

Nick watched a seagull sail over the waves and thought how simple the bird's life must be.

"We went into it with clear boundaries from the start. Nothing serious. Then I changed the rules and asked for more, but she wasn't interested."

"Then she's an idiot," Mia snapped in a show of sibling loyalty. "You're the most caring man she's ever going to meet. You can cook circles around anyone, though I suppose in her case that isn't a bonus. And you're also hot, or so nearly every single female on this island—and a few not-so-single—have pointed out as if I want to hear this about my own brother."

Amused, he said, "I'll take names if you want to share."

"Not a chance. So what's her problem?"

Answering that question would reveal more than Lauren would likely appreciate, so he simply said, "She didn't feel the same. It happens. How about you?"

Dark hair blew across her face and she swiped it away. "How about me what?"

"I shared my story. Now it's your turn. What's going on between you and Henri?"

Her mouth twisted as she brushed nonexistent lint off her pants. "I'm not ready for that."

"Mia, you've been preaching at me for years to start living my life. Maybe it's time to take your own advice."

"My situation is different."

"There's no reason it has to be." Tapping the back of her hand, Nick said, "Nota would never turn her back on you. If Henri can make you happy, then she'll love her for that alone."

"I don't want to disappoint her," she whispered.

"Nota would never be disappointed in you."

Biting her lip, Mia pulled her knees up to her chest. "I'm not talking about Grandma."

So that's how it was. Nick had no idea how to discuss such things with his sister, regardless of what team she played for. Wanting to give her some reply, he offered the one thing he knew for sure.

"You deserve love as much as anyone else," he said. "Don't let fear stand in the way of something good."

When she didn't respond, Nick let the subject drop and together they watched the waves in silence, each wallowing in their own romantic shortcomings.

19

"WHERE DO YOU GET THE INSPIRATION FOR YOUR FOOD?" the reporter asked.

Lauren had already answered this question three times. Thank goodness this was the last interview of the day.

Will had not been kidding about making sure the restaurant had plenty of PR. They'd used the conference room at the Destination Anchor offices as a makeshift media space, and Lauren had been taking time away from the kitchen to be available.

"I grew up around Boston so there's plenty of New England influence," she explained. "Lots of seafood, of course, which is why operating a restaurant here on Anchor Island was a perfect fit. The fresh product so readily available made creating the menu a dream."

"This is your first time running your own kitchen,

correct?" he said, shoving the small recorder closer to her face. Another repeat question.

"Yes, this is my first opportunity to take the lead," she said, repeating what she'd told the previous interviewers, "but I've been in the industry for more than a decade so I'm fully comfortable in the position."

"I was lucky enough to get a table for brunch this morning and I wanted to ask about the baked flounder and eggs combo. Though more common in other parts of the world, what made you put such a unique dish on the menu here?"

At first, the staff had not been in support of the late addition to the menu, but once they'd tasted Lauren's version, they were easily convinced.

"A friend made the dish for me once and I liked it so much I believed that others would as well."

"You were right," he said. "That was one of the best meals I've ever eaten."

Appreciating the high praise, she said, "I'm glad you liked it."

"One more question. What made you come all the way to Anchor Island from Boston? There must have been bigger, more *prestigious* opportunities in the city. So why here?"

Lauren kept the smile on her face while answering what she considered an insulting question, to both the island and the people on it.

"As I'm sure you know, Anchor Island has strict rules regarding what businesses can operate here. They support mom and pop operations and keep big business and franchises out. This policy creates a unique opportunity for creators like me, who have a voice and want to be heard above the noise. An opportunity that would be nearly impossible to find anywhere else."

The reporter snapped off the recorder and shoved the dark-rimmed glasses up his nose. "Great answer. Thanks for taking the time to do this."

"My pleasure," she said, sliding off the high stool, anxious to get back to the restaurant.

"All done?" Roxie asked, popping her head in.

"Yes, we just finished," the reporter replied.

"Then I'll show you out. Lauren, you have one more person to talk to. Hold on and I'll bring him in."

So much for going back to work. With a huff, Lauren pulled out her phone and returned to the stool. She still checked regularly for messages from Nick. In the last ten days she'd gone through what she assumed were all the stages of a breakup. Never having had a relationship meant never having gone through the end of one.

First had been the crying accompanied by lots of ice cream. And then she'd felt like an idiot for being so dramatic and been fine for a couple of days. About day five the anger set in. How dare he not even try to talk to her? Yes, she'd been a jerk. Yes, she'd told him to stop trying to mentor her. She hadn't said she never wanted to speak to him again.

Or had she? Lauren wished she could remember the details from the night she was drunk. Maybe she'd said something that made him think they couldn't even be friends anymore. Between launching the restaurant and sorting out her feelings for Nick—both of which had left her teetering on the edge of a full-blown panic attack—there was no telling what she'd said.

His silence should have been a relief. This was what she wanted. Then again, if she'd really wanted him out of her life, why had she been a hot mess of longing and loneliness and another l-word she would not remotely entertain for the last ten days?

"Here he is," Lauren heard Roxie say right before the conference room door closed. Slipping the phone into her pocket, she stood and turned around, saying, "Hello, I'm Chef Lauren Riley."

"Tell me something I don't know," the man said with a wide grin.

Without thinking, Lauren ran into her brother's arms with tears streaming down her face.

"Hey," Knox said. "I knew you'd be happy to see me, but what's all this about?" Lauren hadn't realized how badly she needed to see a familiar face until that moment. Her brother hugged her tight despite saying, "You're getting my uniform all wet."

Not wanting to make a mess on his Army fatigues, she leaned back, sniffling. "I'm just so happy to see you. But how? I mean, what are you doing here?"

"I couldn't *not* come celebrate my big sis opening her first restaurant," he said. "I'd have been here for day one, but this was the soonest I could get leave."

Lauren couldn't stop staring at him. He looked so good. So healthy and happy. Then she realized how far he'd traveled to be there.

"But you're stationed in Kentucky and the closest airport to Anchor is hours away. How did you even get to the island?"

Knox dabbed at her damp cheeks with his knuckles. "We're in Norfolk for a couple of weeks of training so I just had to rent a car and drive down. I have three days. So when do I get to see this fancy restaurant?"

Flustered, she took his hand. "Now. Of course. We'll go right now."

She dragged him out of the conference room to find Roxie sitting on the corner of her desk with a conspiratorial smile on her face. "Surprised you, huh?"

"You had something to do with this?" Lauren asked.

With a jaunty head tilt, she said, "I might have helped a little."

"I had to find an accomplice if I was going to surprise you." Knox gave Roxie a fist bump. "The directions were perfect, thanks."

"How?" Lauren asked.

"Before the restaurant was open for business, the number here was listed on the website. He called, I answered, and a plan was hatched."

She poked her new friend in the arm. "You kept this a secret from me."

The younger woman walked around to her chair. "I

nearly told you a few days ago when you looked like you needed a pick-me-up, but now I'm glad I didn't."

"I appreciate the self-control," Knox said with a salute.

"Hello," Will said, entering the building. "How did the interviews go?"

"Good, I think." She hoped so anyway. Lauren pulled her brother up beside her and made the introductions. "Will Navarro, this is my brother Knox Riley. Knox, Will and her husband Randy own the restaurant."

Will stopped walking and stared at the newcomer as if she were seeing a ghost. Roxie snapped her fingers in front of her boss' nose.

"Will, are you okay?"

She shook her head. "Yes. Yes, I'm fine." Closing the distance between them, she greeted Knox with an outstretched hand. "It's nice to meet you, Knox. Your sister is doing an amazing job and you should be really proud of her."

"I've always been proud of her," he said, his eyes on Lauren. "I know better than anyone how good she is."

The blush warmed her cheeks. "I was just going to show him the restaurant."

"Could that wait?" Will asked, her eyes cutting to Knox and then back to Lauren. "There's something we need to discuss."

Confused, Lauren said, "Right now?"

Will nodded. "Yes, right now."

She looked at her brother. "Do you mind waiting?"

"No problem. We can head over when you're done."

"I'll keep him company," Roxie said. "Maybe I can get him to share some stories from when you were kids."

The stories from Lauren and Knox's childhood weren't the type Roxie was likely hoping for. She gave Knox a *don't tell too much* look before following Will into the conference room. When her boss closed the door, Lauren's heart sank to her knees. Had she done something wrong? Were they not happy with the restaurant? Pilar's had been open less than two weeks. Surely they would give her more time than that before deciding to replace her.

"Have a seat." Will sat down at the head of the table and pulled an envelope from her bag. Setting it in front of her, she waited for Lauren to sit before saying, "This is for you, but I need to explain something first."

Lauren's palms began to sweat and she shoved her hands under her thighs. "Okay."

"Does the name Van Clement mean anything to you?"

Lauren sat up straighter. "That's the name of a family my mom worked for when I was a kid."

"So you know about them?"

"They're one of the wealthiest families in Boston. Everyone knows about them."

Will blew out a breath and said, "I'm a Van Clement."

Struggling to keep her jaw off the table, Lauren said, "*You're* a Van Clement?"

"Yes," she replied. "Though I didn't grow up with the

family. My mother ran away when she was pregnant with me and it wasn't until I was twenty-five that she told me the truth."

Who would run away from a life of money and privilege? "Then you're rich," Lauren said. "I mean, I knew you were Anchor Island rich, considering you own multiple businesses and you haven't batted an eye at anything I've requested for Pilar's, but the Van Clements are like, one-percenter rich."

"I inherited the estate seven years ago."

Feeling like a peasant among royalty, Lauren crossed her arms. "Lucky you."

"Did your mother ever mention Brandon Van Clement?" Will asked.

Lauren had no idea where this was going.

"She stopped working for the family when I was five. I doubt she'd have mentioned anyone to me by name, and if she did, I wouldn't remember them now." The wealthy weren't nearly as important as they liked to think. "Why are you asking me these questions? If you think Mom stole something, I know she didn't."

Lauren knew no such thing, but if her mother did steal something of value, she'd done it to take care of them. Maybe if the family had paid her a living wage, she wouldn't have had to steal to feed her children.

Will remained calm. "I'm not accusing your mom of anything, Lauren. I'm asking because Brandon Van Clement, my uncle, was your father."

That could not be true. "You're out of your mind,"

she said, bolting from her chair. "My father was a janitor who cut out before I was born. Mom told me so herself. Whoever told you this crazy story was lying."

Holding Lauren's gaze, Will slid the envelope across the table. "I think it's time for you to read this."

Looking at the offering as if it might explode, she said, "What is it?"

"A letter from your mother."

Lauren fell back into her chair as the breath left her body. She stared at the envelope, trying to make sense of what Will was saying. Why would Will have a letter from her mother?

"That can't be."

"Once you read the letter, I'll explain everything."

There couldn't possibly be an explanation because none of this made any sense. Mom died in October and Lauren had never even heard of Will Navarro or this island until February.

"I don't know what's in that envelope, but it can't be for me."

Will pushed it closer. "Rosemary asked me to give this to you. I understand that this is a lot, and you have every right to be suspicious, but I'm trying to honor her wishes. Please, Lauren, just read the letter."

Hands shaking, she picked up the envelope and withdrew the paper inside, recognizing her mother's handwriting instantly. Throat tight, she blinked away tears in order to focus on the words.

"Here," Will said, passing her a box of tissues.

Lauren dried her eyes and read.

Dear Lauren,

I'm sure this is coming as a surprise, but I wanted to take this last chance to do for you now what I should have done a long time ago. You turned out to be an amazing woman, and I still have no idea how that happened. It sure as hell isn't because of me. Instead of being there for you and being a real mom, I was out chasing the next man or the next high or both. I know you still have Knox, but you were always more a mother to him than I was, and he's off playing war or whatever it is he does in that Army. He can't be around to make sure you're looked after. To make sure you aren't left alone in the world like I was.

Ms. Navarro probably told you by now, but your father is Brandon Van Clement. He's Knox's father, too. Before you get all angry, thinking he's some horrible bastard, know that I never told him. His family wouldn't have let him marry a woman like me, and I made sure he thought I was out sleeping with other men so he wouldn't get suspicious. You see, if he'd known, he'd have taken you kids away from me. Goodness knows he'd have had the right, considering what a mess I was. But I was selfish and didn't want to be alone. Funny how that turned out.

Anyway, when I knew I didn't have much longer to go, I looked him up and found out that he died a few months ago. Well, a few months before I'm writing this. That led me to Ms. Navarro, so I sent her a letter asking her to find a way to make sure you were taken care of. I want you to get your dream of having your own kitchen, and I thought maybe she knew somebody who could make that happen. She told me that she would take care of it, and if you're reading this, then that means she stuck to her word. Thank her for me.

I didn't want you to know all of this until you'd gotten your dream. The one thing we have in common is pride, and I was afraid you wouldn't take the job if you thought I'd used some piddly last wish to get it for you. I'm sure that by now you're knocking it out of the park, and I want you to know that I'm watching you, the proudest mom on both heaven and earth.

I love you, baby. I didn't say that often enough, and I didn't come close to showing it, but for my whole life, you were and will always be my greatest achievement. I hope you're happy, and I hope you've surrounded yourself with people who care about you. Don't ever take that for granted, and whatever you do, don't make the same mistakes that I did. Laugh and love and let people see how great you are.

Have a wonderful life, my sweet baby girl.

Love,

Mom

Lauren held the wadded-up tissue against her lips as she stared at the letter in her hand. She was crying hard enough to give herself hiccups so the words were a blur, but she couldn't put the paper down. This was her last connection to the most important woman in her life. The woman she'd known to be imperfect, but still loved more than anything. The woman who had been Lauren's only anchor is a world full of chaos and confusion.

It hadn't mattered that Mom was the source of that

chaos. That, as she admitted, she hadn't been the greatest parent. She'd been the *only* parent. Who else was Lauren going to look up to? Take her life lessons from?

...don't make the same mistakes that I did.

Was she doing that? Lauren didn't bounce around from man to man, but she'd left one job after another. She didn't twist herself into a person she wasn't to get attention, but she had suppressed every facet of her personality so as not to be noticed. Different methods, but the same result. Like her mother, she was alone.

"When did she give this to you?" Lauren asked once she was able to breathe again.

"It arrived a few days after our last phone call. She wanted to make sure I would do as she'd asked."

"She says to thank you."

Will smiled for the first time since they'd entered the room. "She's most welcome, but I should be thanking her. She gave me an amazingly talented chef to run my restaurant."

"Did you buy Pilar's for me?"

"No. Randy and I had already put in an offer, but before your mother found me, we had no plans to revamp it. I'm glad that changed." Reaching into the bag beside her chair, she pulled out a small satin pouch and slid it toward Lauren. "This came with the letter. She told me during that last phone call that she was sending something that had belonged to her mother. I assume this is it."

Not sure how much more she could take, Lauren eased the pouch open and a cameo dropped onto her palm. The background was a rich mustard yellow, and the delicate and feminine silhouette looked to be cut out of ivory. There was no way to tell the age, but the bauble was well cared for and made to be worn as either a broach or on a chain.

"I've never seen this before."

"I've seen something similar," Will replied. "Most likely nineteenth century. It's very valuable."

Lauren twirled the trinket in her hand, wondering why Mom had never mentioned it. And then a realization dawned. All those years of barely getting by, working multiple jobs just so they could eat, Mom had held on to something that could have easily been pawned for a quick meal. She must have truly cherished the delicate heirloom to keep it through so much struggle.

"I'm sorry that I didn't tell you before now," Will said, "but she made me promise to wait. I was surprised out there when I first came in because your brother looks exactly like Uncle Brandon. Not that I doubted your mother, but if I had, seeing him would have convinced me."

"Wait," Lauren said. "Does this mean that we're cousins?"

Will nodded. "It does. Welcome to the family, Lauren."

20

NICK TOSSED THE CHICKEN INTO THE GARBAGE WITH A muffled curse. He'd trashed three in the last hour and was seriously considering *not* entering the damn Best of the Fest contest. He'd won it twice. What would it matter if he let someone else have it this year? With two days to go, he still had no idea what he was going to cook, and backing out would make his life that much easier.

"The packet for the food festival is here," said Patty Dempsey as she stepped out of the back office. "We've got the layout for the tents so we can see how the diners will move through."

The order of the tents was very important. Too close to the front and the diners were likely to forget your food by the time they tasted all of the others. Too far in the back and there was a chance their palates would be blown out before they reached you. A dish could be the best food ever, but that didn't matter if the diner couldn't taste it.

One spicy dish could put every vendor after out of the running.

"Did we get our regular spot?" Nick asked.

Patty slid reading glasses onto her nose. "We did, and it's even better this year since it's right next to Pilar's."

Not what Nick wanted to hear. "Do you think they'd move us?"

The older woman stared over her glasses. "Why would we want to be moved? Pilar's is the most popular eatery on this island right now. Everyone in attendance will want to check them out, especially since getting a table is nearly impossible. That will bring even more people our way."

And put Lauren directly in his path. After Mia left that morning, Nick had pulled up Lauren's number in his phone. He'd written and deleted four different messages before once again staring at a blank screen. And then he did what he should have done a week ago. He deleted her number.

"Sounds more like we'll get overshadowed," he said, searching for any excuse she might accept.

His boss arched a brow. "Are you suggesting our food isn't good enough to compete with Pilar's?"

The two menus weren't even in the same ballpark, and Nick had no insecurities about his food. He also had no intention of telling Patty the real reason he wanted the tent moved.

"This isn't about the food. The draw for Pilar's is that they're new and have a lot of buzz. Their like a novelty act at a circus. Once the fascination dies down, the crowds disappear, but by the time that happens, they've overlooked the acts that are actually worth their while."

"What exactly are you saying?" Patty asked, brows drawn.

Nick had no idea. "Forget it," he said, swiping the towel off his shoulder and wiping his hands. "I've decided to skip Best of the Fest this year and let someone else have a shot."

"Since when? We're days away and the entry fee has been paid."

"I'm sure you can get the money back. If not, take it out of my pay."

He didn't want to compete knowing that Lauren wouldn't have the same opportunity. The truth was, she deserved the prize. Pilar's was popular for a reason, and that reason was *her* food.

"I don't do this very often," Patty said, "but I'm overruling you. Dempsey's is going to compete this weekend, even if that means one of the other cooks has to take the lead. Is that what you want?"

This was his kitchen and if a dish went into that contest, he would be the one to make it.

"No, ma'am," he said through clenched teeth. "I'll do it."

"Good." She dropped the packet on the corner of the prep station. "We have until tomorrow afternoon to submit the name of the dish. Fill this out and I'll email it over."

Nick nodded and Patty returned to her office. So much for saving himself the hassle. Ignoring the packet, he stomped off to the cooler to see what he had available. When he spotted the fresh tuna delivered that morning, an idea bloomed. He knew the perfect way to follow his boss' order and appease his own conscience.

———

"I CAN'T BELIEVE she kept this secret our whole lives," Knox said, staring at the letter in his hand.

Once they'd shared the story with her brother, Will had suggested Lauren take the rest of the day off so the two of them could spend some time processing what they'd learned. She'd been through something similar in her twenties and knew how overwhelming this revelation could be. The sky was the perfect shade of blue as they sat on Lauren's small back deck and tried to take it all in.

"At least she didn't take the secret to her grave," Lauren replied. "Not that this does us much good now, since he's gone too, but it's nice to know the truth."

"She told us we had two *different* dads. I've never thought of you as anything less than my full sister, but how could you tell your kids a lie like that?"

Lauren and Knox were having very different responses to the news. Where she understood now how much their mother's choices revealed what her children had meant to her, Knox was angry that she'd deprived them of knowing their father and of having a better life.

Lauren couldn't blame him. There'd been days when they'd struggled to scrounge up a single meal, yet one phone call would have meant never going hungry again. There was a selfishness to Mom's actions that was hard to forgive. But she'd also worked her fingers to the bone to make sure they were never homeless, that they had clothes on their backs and a roof over their heads.

The clothes were threadbare and the roof had a hole from time to time, but they'd never had to live in a box or sleep in a shelter. That isn't a high bar to set for a parent, but somehow knowing that Mom's life might have been easier without them in it said a lot about how far she went to keep them close.

"You read the letter. If she'd told us the truth, she might have lost us."

"If she'd told us the truth, we could have had a real childhood. Think of what she took from us. Our own rooms. Regular meals. I could have played ball and been a normal kid."

He was right. And yet Lauren couldn't help but defend her.

"Do you think growing up as a Van Clement would have been normal? Especially if the other rich kids found out that our mom had once been the help?"

Knox ran a hand over his short hair. "I'd rather have

food in my belly and be an outsider than go through what we endured."

Lauren hadn't realized how much their experience had affected him. Her little brother had been an easygoing kid. As happy as any child could be in their situation. He'd kept his head down in school, gotten good grades, and planned a future in the military from the age of fourteen.

"I wish things had been different for both of us," she said, taking his hand. "But we can't change the past. I think her goal with all of this was to maybe change our futures. We have a family now."

Saying the words helped Lauren realize that she'd found a family even before Will had given her the letter. The staff in the kitchen had all become important to her. Roxie, who'd barreled into her life and declared them friends that day in the office, no longer had to coerce her to go places. The restaurant kept her busy, but Lauren had managed to keep up with the Tuesday ladies' nights. She even liked playing with the little ones.

Then there was Nick.

"Am I repeating her mistakes?" Lauren asked.

"Why would you ask that? Of course not."

She wasn't so sure. "In the letter, she said she doesn't want me to be alone. All this time, I thought that was the goal."

Knox leaned forward. "What are you talking about? You aren't alone. You have me."

Lauren offered a crooked smile. "I know I do, but

you can't be around all the time, and you shouldn't have to be. You have your own life to live."

"But you have people around you, right? Friends?" He twisted the hat in his hands. "I haven't even asked if you have a boyfriend. Is there someone I get to meet while I'm here? Someone I get to scare into taking good care of you?"

There could have been. Ten days ago.

"I have a few friends, but only because the people on this island have a way of pulling you in. I did my best to keep them at a distance, but they wore me down, I guess."

"Why would you want to keep them at a distance?"

Clearly, they'd gotten two different messages growing up. "Do you remember Mom saying never to depend on anyone?"

"No" he said, shaking his head. "All I ever got was *don't be an asshole.*"

Annoyed that he didn't remember, she scooted to the edge of her seat. "She said it all the time. Don't depend on anyone because they'll always let you down. That was like, her mantra."

"Then she should have practiced what she preached. Every time one guy left her, she'd hop to the next. That one would steal all of our furniture, and she'd have another loser by the end of the week." His eyes scanned the horizon. "If anything, she depended on too many people. She just couldn't pick a good one to save her life. Or ours."

How had Lauren never made that connection? The slew of men moving in and out of their lives wasn't the problem. It was a natural result of the real problem— that Mom couldn't stand to be alone, even if it meant dating complete jerks. Or lying to her children about who their father was.

"Knox, I think I might have really messed up."

"Messed up what?" he asked.

"Remember that boyfriend question?"

"Yeah. Are you dating someone?"

Bolting from her chair, Lauren unzipped her oversized jacket on her way inside. "Give me an hour, and then we're going out to eat."

Knox stood up. "You mean to Pilar's? Do I need to change my uniform?"

"Not Pilar's," she said, hoping she hadn't waited too long. "And there's no need for you to change. I just need to look better than..." She glanced down at her ripped jeans and dirty Chucks. "This."

"So you *are* seeing someone," he said with a chuckle.

"If I'm lucky, I will be after tonight."

———

BY THE END of his shift, the competition dish had been perfected, though he'd had to reach out to a friend for one of the ingredients. Jackson had come through, as always. In a moment of weakness, Nick had asked about Lauren and learned that she'd been busy doing publicity for the restaurant, which was doing better than anyone could have hoped.

He wished he could tell her how proud he was. Less than six weeks ago, she'd been in over her head with no idea how to open a restaurant. Nick had given her a push here and there, but *she'd* made it happen. The menu, which was fresh and original, highlighting local ingredients with her own New England flare, was unlike anything he'd seen before. That she'd taught the staff how to create those flavors in such a short time said a lot about how good she really was.

"Nick, someone is asking to see the chef," Georgette called into the kitchen as he untied his apron. No one called him chef around here, so it had to be some tourist unhappy with their food. Every once in a while they'd get an out-of-towner who didn't like a sauce or complained that his burger had extra stuff on it. As if the description wasn't printed right there on the menu.

"I'm off the clock," he called back. "Let Carl handle it."

Carl Oliver had been part of the crew since before Nick took over and he'd always been more patient with the customers.

"They asked specifically for you," she answered.

So not a tourist then.

Tossing the apron in the hamper in the back, he grabbed his jacket off the hook and headed for the swinging door. When he reached the dining room, he spotted Lauren standing by the entrance talking to a tall man in fatigues. White-blond hair hung in loose curls around her face, and the blue and white dress clung to her curves, then billowed out to stop just above her knees. She was bouncing on the balls of her feet and smiling up at the man like a woman in love.

He couldn't believe she'd bring a date to Dempsey's.

Anger rising, Nick sought out Georgette and found her at the other end of the bar. "Who asked to see me?"

"The new chef," she answered, loading three tall necks onto her tray. "She's over by the door."

This could not be happening. Why would Lauren ask to see him while out with another man? Glancing their way, he watched the soldier drop a kiss on top of her head and he'd never felt the urge to kill a man more.

Determined to get this over with, Nick charged through the thin crowd to reach his target.

"You asked for me?" he said, skipping the niceties.

Lauren looked up, startled, her blue eyes going soft as they fell on his face. "Hi."

That was it? She'd asked for him to say hello?

"I was heading home. What did you want?"

"Are you sure this is the guy?" the soldier mumbled, but Lauren ignored him.

"Then you aren't working?" she asked.

"I just finished for the day."

"Could we sit down and talk?"

As if he had any intention of being her third wheel.

"Looks like you already have a dinner partner," he

replied, casting a snarl in the stranger's direction. "Have a nice night."

"Wait," she said as he tried to pass. "This is my brother. He came to visit to help celebrate the launch of Pilar's." *Her brother?* "Knox Riley, this is Nick Stamatis," she continued. "He's the head chef here at Dempsey's and was helpful in getting Pilar's up and running."

Still stunned by the introduction, Nick said, "I didn't do much. Did you say brother?"

Lauren nodded as the smile on her face widened. "I did. I wanted the two of you to meet. Are you sure you don't have time to sit down?"

More than a little off-balance, he rubbed the back of his neck. "I've got a few minutes." Looking around, he said, "Annie, is table seventeen open?"

She checked the chart on the podium and said, "Yes, sir."

Nick led Lauren and her brother through the tables to the booth in the far corner. When he gestured for them to sit, Lauren slid in first and the soldier followed. Nick took a seat on the opposite side.

"Knox, is it?" he asked.

"That's right." The brother, a large man with a square jaw and a crew cut, extended a hand. "Lauren told me a lot about you on the way over."

Unsure if what he'd heard had been good or bad, Nick accepted the greeting in silence.

"How are you?" Lauren asked, as if they were old friends catching up.

"Busy planning for the festival. I assume you've been busy, too."

Too busy to pick up a phone or send a message.

"Yes, I have. We're nearly sold out for every seating."

"So I hear."

An awkward silence loomed until Knox said, "I'm going to the bar for a beer. Can I get you anything, Nick?"

He shook his head. "No, I'm good."

"How about you, sis?"

"I'm okay." As her brother crossed the room, Lauren watched him with pride in her eyes. A second later, she turned her attention back to Nick. "I apologize for taking so long."

Feeling like a man caught in the crosshairs, Nick's body tensed. "So long for what?"

"To give you an answer."

Now he was truly confused.

"You already gave me your answer on that," Nick said. "Followed by ten days of silence to drive the message home."

Lauren didn't blame him for being mad, though she hoped there was some hurt as well. That would mean he still cared.

"I'd like to take that answer back."

"Pretending I'd agree to that, why?"

She'd been formulating this speech from the moment she'd stepped into the shower, but she was struggling to remember the words now.

"Because I've had time to think about it some more and my answer has changed."

Brown eyes narrowed. "That isn't what I mean. Why has it changed?"

This was already not going to plan. Taking a deep breath, she tried again.

"What I'm about to tell you is not an excuse for how I've hurt you, but it will give some context for my answer. I mentioned in the past that I had to take care of Knox from a young age, and that we never knew our fathers. Well, father, now, but that's another story. Anyway, the truth is that we were really poor, we moved around *a lot*—usually because we were evicted for not paying rent—and Mom fell into one bad relationship after another."

She took a breath, mustering up the courage to say the rest.

"The lesson I took from all of that was that letting people get close to me would mean getting hurt. Men left—or sometimes they sucked you dry, stole all of your stuff, and then left—but the bottom line was don't trust and you'll be safe. What I didn't realize is that not everyone is like those people Mom brought home. That trust isn't always used as a weapon, and letting someone in can actually be a good thing. You taught me that, but it wasn't until today that the message sunk in."

Nick leaned back with an unreadable expression. The longer he remained silent, the faster her heart beat.

"I understand if it's too late," she said, "but I wanted you to know all of this either way. I don't remember much about that last night, so I don't honestly know what answer I gave you. Since I haven't heard from you—"

"Since you haven't heard from me?" he cut in. "Are you saying you didn't want this to end?"

"I just didn't want to get hurt," she replied. "But being scared is no excuse for the way—"

Before she could finish the sentence, Nick was on his feet and tugging her into his arms. Without another word, his lips were on hers and all she could do was hold on as the kiss turned her bones to jelly. Not until he finally pulled away did Lauren realize the other diners were applauding.

Cheeks hot from both arousal and embarrassment, she buried her face in his shoulder as a roomful of strangers whistled and cheered in support of a love story they knew nothing about. Happier than she could ever remember being, Lauren looked up into warm brown eyes and a little voice said, "Don't mess this up again."

Laying her cheek against Nick's chest, she whispered, "I won't, Mom. I promise."

"What was that?" Nick said, nudging her head up with a gentle touch of her chin.

"I was just saying thank you."

"No, thank you." He kissed the tip of her nose. "I thought I lost you for good."

She'd been lost all right. For much longer than the last ten days.

"Looks like we might have something to celebrate," Knox said, returning to the table. He held a bottle of champagne in one hand and three glasses in the other. "This seemed more appropriate than a beer."

Lauren laughed and let go of Nick long enough to

kiss her brother on the cheek. "I am definitely ready to celebrate." Turning back to Nick, she added, "It isn't every day a girl realizes that she's fallen in love."

Nick kissed her once more, eliciting more oohs and aahs from the crowd, then he pulled away, flashed a crooked grin, and said, "I'm glad you're finally catching up."

———

NICK COULDN'T BELIEVE she was back in his arms.

Lauren curled up tighter against him, sighing as she slid her soft calf along his. "Do I want to know what I said that night?" she whispered.

He rubbed his thumb along her shoulder. "You said you didn't like needing me and that you were sure I'd walk away." Turning to kiss her forehead, Nick said, "I'll never do that."

"I should have been braver," she mumbled into his chest.

"You are brave. It takes guts to go your own way. To move to a new place to chase a dream. Not a lot of people would do that."

"That isn't the same, though. I'm talking about us."

Tucking her beneath his chin, Nick watched the ceiling fan spin in the dark. "You came back to me. That's all that matters."

Twirling a finger through his chest hair, she said, "I never would have guessed how much coming to this island would change my life. I found you, and now I have a cousin and a whole new family to learn about."

Confused, he said, "A new family?"

"Oh, I haven't told you that yet, have I?" Lauren leaned up on an elbow. "Will Navarro is my cousin."

"How did that happen?"

"Her uncle is mine and Knox's biological father, though he apparently never knew that we were his. Before she died, Mom tried to track him down and the hunt led her to Will. That's how I ended up here. Mom's last wish was for me to get my dream, and since she knew Will is super rich… Do people here know how rich she is?"

Nick knew the Navarros were successful business owners, but he'd never heard the term *super rich* tossed around. "What exactly qualifies as super rich?" he asked.

She narrowed her eyes. "Like not quite Bill Gates, but a level above Beyoncé."

"Seriously?"

"The Van Clement family is old money in Boston," she said, lying back down. "I've grown to like this island, but if you saw the mansion Will *could* be living in, you'd wonder what the hell she's thinking staying here."

He'd had no idea and wondered if anyone else did.

"So that's how I ended up here. Mom asked her if she knew a way for me to get my own restaurant. Will told me today that they hadn't intended to revamp the Marina after buying it, but to grant Mom's wish, they put the plan into motion, found me, and here I am."

Then that was why Will hired such an inexperienced chef. "Did she recruit you, then? Didn't you wonder why she'd contacted you out of nowhere?"

"She was smarter than that," Lauren explained. "Mom told her I'd never take the job if I knew the truth, so Will contacted my boss and asked him to pass me the job info but to make it look like he'd told everyone."

"And you didn't think twice about applying?" he asked. "This isn't exactly a short trip from Boston."

Lauren rolled onto her back and crossed her arms over the top of the sheet. "To be honest, I'm not sure what possessed me to do it. When I applied, I didn't really expect anything to come of it." Looking his way, she added, "I definitely didn't expect to come here and fall in love."

Leaning over her, Nick trailed a finger along her cheek. "That's the second time you've said that. Do you really love me?"

With a nod, she said, "I know it's too fast, and I don't expect you to feel the same way."

"I love you, Lauren." Relief softened her features and he wanted to keep her looking that happy for the rest of his life. "I love your strength, your determination, and most of all, I love that you have no idea how special you are."

"I feel special when I'm with you." Pulling him to her, she pressed her lips to his and Nick shifted until she was under him. Breaking the kiss, she stared into his eyes and whispered, "Don't ever let me go."

"Never," he replied.

———

"COME ON," Lauren said, tugging Roxie through the crowd. "They're about to announce the winner. I don't want to miss it."

"I'm going as fast as I can," her friend said. "We already know he's going to win."

"That's why I can't miss it."

Due to running her own tent, Lauren hadn't seen Nick since they'd woken up that morning and dashed around each other to get ready. Despite her barrage of questions, he'd refused to tell her anything about the dish he'd entered in the festival competition. Though she was happy that Pilar's was so popular, that popularity had made leaving the tent to taste anyone else's food impossible to do.

Lauren had given up any concern about entering the contest, since Pilar's was already filled to capacity every shift. What she'd always thought was a competitive nature had turned out to be more about survival than winning. Now that she was content for quite possibly the first time in her life, the need to prove herself and her food had disappeared.

"There's Jackson," she said, spotting the tall black man at the front of the crowd. "We need to get up there."

"Cut around here," Roxie said, pointing to an opening along the side.

They followed that path and reached her coworker at the same time that Will walked onto the makeshift stage. The competing chefs were lined up along the back, and Lauren caught sight of Nick in the lineup. She'd never seen him in a chef's jacket before. Good Lord, he looked hot. He also looked nervous, which surprised her. She didn't have to know what he'd cooked to know that he was the best chef up there.

"Welcome to the final event of this year's Anchor Island Food Festival," her cousin said into the microphone. "We've hit record attendance numbers this year, and thanks to the amazing eateries up and down the coast, the food has been better than ever. I speak for the planning committee and the entire island when I say thank you all for coming, and thanks to everyone who brought their delicious food for us to try."

The crowd applauded, with a few louder whistles coming from the back, and Will waited for the cheers to fade before speaking again.

"The competition for Best of the Fest was tough, as always, but the votes have been counted and it's my pleasure to announce the winner." She paused to open a small envelope in her hand. Withdrawing the card inside, her smile widened as she said, "The winner of Best of the Fest for the third year in a row is Nick Stamatis of Dempsey's Bar & Grill."

Lauren screamed with excitement, leaping up and down and nearly jerking Roxie's arm off. Then she found herself caught up in a celebratory hug with

Jackson. As Nick took the microphone, she dropped to her feet and shushed those around her so she wouldn't miss a word.

"Thank you, Will," Nick said, accepting the trophy with much more calm than Lauren had displayed. "Thank you to everyone who voted for my dish, but in truth, you really voted for someone else's."

The crowd went quiet as people looked to their neighbors in confusion.

"Lauren, where are you?" Nick said, scanning the audience.

"Here she is," Jackson yelled, while Roxie jumped up and down with a hand in the air.

"What's he doing?" Lauren asked her second-in-command, but all he did was grin in response. Before she knew it, Jackson had shoved her up the stairs beside the stage and she found herself staring at hundreds of questioning eyes.

"Come over here, hon," Nick said.

Unable to do anything else, she closed the distant between them and leaned against his side. "What are you doing?" she whispered.

Nick ignored the question. "As most of you probably know, this is Lauren Riley, the head chef of Pilar's here on the island. Due to Will Navarro, the event coordinator, being the owner of that establishment, Lauren was shut out of the competition."

"You don't need to do this," she said, tugging on his sleeve.

He kept going. "I knew I couldn't change that, but what I could do was make sure her food was represented. The dish I made today—tuna steak in a red wine sauce with celery root-potato puree and Brussels sprouts in garlic—is the first dish she ever made for me, and this award belongs to her."

He extended the trophy as the room erupted, the deafening applause making her ears ring.

"I can't," she said, shaking her head. "You made the dish."

"But you created it," Nick replied. "This belongs to you. The best chef here."

As tears filled her eyes, Lauren wrapped her arms around his middle and hid her face in his white jacket. The crowd started chanting, "Speech! Speech!"

Wiping her face, she sniffled as he handed her the microphone. The audience grew quiet once more and she took a deep breath, stalling for time.

"Hello," she finally muttered. "I'm a bit speechless since I didn't expect to be up here today. I guess I should say thank you to everyone who voted for the dish, though that feels weird since I'm not the one who made it." Quiet laughter rippled through the crowd. "I'm not sure how I got lucky enough to land on this amazing little island, but I'm really happy that I did. And I'm looking forward to making food here for years to come."

More cheers filled the large tent as Lauren handed the microphone back to Will before dragging Nick to the side of the stage. "I can't believe you did that."

"You put my dish on your menu," he reminded her. "Turnabout is fair play." Sobering, he kissed her knuckles. "I entered this dish before you came back to me. I meant it when I said your food deserved to be represented here."

She couldn't believe he would have done this even if she'd never come to her senses.

"Thank you. I can't tell you how much that means to me."

With a twinkle in his eye, he said, "You'll have to show me then."

Her laughter danced around them. "Oh, yes. That I can do."

EPILOGUE

LAUREN COULDN'T BELIEVE PILAR'S HAD BEEN OPEN FOR A full month and they had yet to see a drop in business. If anything, they'd gotten busier with every passing day to the point that a new patio section was currently under construction along the back of the building. The covered area would offer amazing views of the sound and the ocean beyond, and could be closed up in winter for year-round use.

The staff worked like a dream, with or without her, and Lauren was enjoying a little extra time to explore her new home. The lighthouse was, in fact, as short and fat as Mia had painted it to be. The Blackbeard museum was both cheesy and educational—if you didn't mind the swashbuckling tour guide calling you matey for an hour. And nearly every island local greeted her by name when they crossed paths, often stopping to chat about whatever dish at Pilar's they'd most recently tried.

Even when she had someplace to be, Lauren didn't mind taking an extra few minutes for the brief encounters. As Nick once said, on Anchor Island, you really do have all the time in the world.

To celebrate Pilar's one-month milestone, the pre-launch dinner group had been invited back, only this time Lauren joined them for the meal. Everyone got to order their own favorite, and conversations around the table were boisterous in some cases, more moderate in others. The children were back, of course, and this time the twins were in attendance.

Lauren couldn't remember ever holding a baby so small.

"Aren't they precious?" Roxie said, staring into the chubby little face of baby Roxanne. Apparently, Roxie had taken care of Callie while she'd been on bed rest for weeks before giving birth, and her generosity had been rewarded by gaining her own namesake.

"They're beautiful," Lauren agreed. She had the pleasure of holding baby Rachel, who squirmed and gurgled before settling to gnaw on one tiny knuckle.

Mia leaned over Roxie's shoulder and said, "They're getting so big."

This was big? How small were they before?

The women continued to coo over the infants until Henri said, "Let me hold my baby cousins before I go."

"Go?" Mia said.

The blonde sat down beside Lauren, who reluctantly handed the baby over.

"I'm leaving the island," Henri said, smiling at the bundle in her arms. "It's conference season. I have reader events throughout the summer."

Lauren didn't have much time for reading, but she'd loaded several of Henri's books onto her phone. Halfway through the first in a small town series, she couldn't wait to find out how the brooding former soldier was going to win the heart of the single mom next door.

"When will you be back?" Mia asked, taking the empty seat beside Roxie.

Henri looked up. "Why?"

An odd question. Lauren looked to Roxie to see if she'd also picked up on the unexpected tension, but the other woman was too focused on the baby to notice.

Mia cast Lauren an uncomfortable glance before saying, "I'm just curious."

"I didn't think you'd care," the author replied.

As if sensing his sister needed rescuing, Nick appeared out of nowhere. "Is this the baby section?" he asked.

Baby Rachel began to fuss, which triggered the same reaction in her sister. Without another word, Henri took the baby back to her mother, and Roxie followed behind her.

"You okay?" Nick asked Mia.

His sister nodded. "Sure. Why wouldn't I be?" Arms crossed over her middle, she glanced around as if seeking an escape hatch. "I'm going to check on Grandma."

As Mia walked away, Nick moved her empty chair closer to Lauren and sat down, sliding an arm around her shoulders.

"Do you want to tell me what that was?" she asked.

Nick sighed. "I think it's time I should, but this has to stay between us."

Concerned, she said, "Of course."

With a nod toward his sister's retreating form, he said, "Mia is gay, but she doesn't think Nota will approve so she keeps it a secret."

Putting two and two together, Lauren said, "And Henri…?"

"Is interested," he said, glancing over to the writer. "Mia won't act on it though, at least not publicly. I have no idea what's happened between them in private."

If that exchange was any indication, feelings are definitely involved.

"What do you think Nota would say?" she asked.

The older woman had been ecstatic to learn that Nick and Lauren were now a couple, and had not hesitated to toss out an I told you so to her grandson. But Lauren hadn't spent much time with her and couldn't begin to guess what her feelings might be about learning her granddaughter was a lesbian.

Nick shrugged. "I honestly don't think she'd care, but she also comes from another generation, when stuff like that was kept quiet if ever talked about at all. Seeing Mia happy is what's important, so I have to think she'd come around. Eventually."

He was probably right, but eventually could be a week or it could be years. Poor Mia. Hiding such a big part of herself could not be easy.

"I wish there was something we could do, but I guess with Henri leaving, there's no point now."

"You never know," Nick said, pressing a kiss against Lauren's temple. "So long as Callie is here, Henri will be back. Maybe Mia will figure it out."

Leaning into him, she said, "I hope so. Now that I know what being in love feels like, I highly recommend it."

"You do, huh?"

"I do," Lauren replied, turning to face him. "I'm glad that Nota convinced you that you aren't going to die anytime soon." Nick had told her the full story about why he'd enacted his no relationships policy. If his grandmother hadn't changed his mind, Lauren would still be as lonely as ever. "And that you didn't give up on me."

Rubbing a thumb along her jaw, he whispered, "Never."

He sealed the vow with a kiss that curled her toes and Lauren knew she would never be lonely again.

———

THANK you so much for reading In Over Her Head. I hope you enjoyed the story and that you might take the time to post a review on Amazon. I would be most grateful, but I'm also grateful that with so many books to choose from, you chose one of mine.

IF YOU LIKE this one enough to try another, make sure you hop over to Amazon now and pre-order the next installment in the series, Christmas On Anchor Island, coming Oct 25, 2021.

ACKNOWLEDGMENTS

Thank you to the fabulous writer Nicki Salcedo for sharing her team building experiences with me. She started the conversation by saying how awful it was, then shared all of the parts she enjoyed. That was exactly what I needed to create the scenes that brought Lauren and her team together. The park that I call Defying Gravity Adventure Park is based on the very real First Flight Adventure Park in Nags Head, NC. There are amazing videos and images on their website so if you want to see what Lauren and her team endured definitely check it out.

Thank you to Kimberly Dawn Edits for being my lovely copyeditor once again. I couldn't possibly do this without you. And a big shout out to Kim Law, who helped me brainstorm this story and even made it possible for us to do so while at the beach. That trip was the highlight of a really crappy year. (All covid precautions were taken so no worries there.)

Anchor Island is affectionately based on the very real Ocracoke Island at the base of the Outer Banks in North Carolina. I couldn't possibly have known when I visited way back in 2007 that this island would change my life so drastically. If you're wishing you could visit Anchor Island, definitely book a trip to Ocracoke. If you do, I hope you'll send me pictures of your adventures!

ABOUT THE AUTHOR

Terri Osburn writes contemporary romance with heart, hope, and lots of humor. After landing on the bestseller lists with her Anchor Island Series, she moved on to the Ardent Springs series, which earned her a Book Buyers Best award in 2016. Terri's work has been translated into five languages, and has sold more than one and a half million copies worldwide. She resides in middle Tennessee with four frisky felines and two high-maintenance terrier mixes. Learn more about this author and her books at www.terriosburn.com. Or check out her Facebook page at www.facebook.com/TerriOsburnAuthor.

Made in USA - Kendallville, IN
1235451_9780998524696
02.17.2021 1231